MASTERS OF THE SKIES

By

Cameron Deakin Moon

This is a work of fiction. Names, characters, places, and incidents are products of the author's imagination or are used fictitiously and are not to be construed as real. Any resemblance to actual events, locations, organizations, or person, living or dead, is entirely coincidental.

WCP

World Castle Publishing, LLC
Pensacola, Florida

Copyright © Cameron Deakin Moon 2014
Print ISBN: 9781629891026
eBook ISBN: 9781629891033
First Edition World Castle Publishing, LLC, June 15, 2014
http://www.worldcastlepublishing.com

Licensing Notes

Cover: Fantasia Frog Designs
Editor: Maxine Bringenberg

Author's Note

This story was inspired by the Legend of Oda Nobunaga.

The story goes, Nobunaga Oda was born June 23, 1534 and supposedly died June 21, 1582. He was murdered by one of his generals, Mitsuhide Akechi, who burned down Honnoji Temple with Nobunaga still inside. The exact reasons for Mitsuhide's betrayal remain a mystery. Some say Mitsuhide betrayed Nobunaga because of the great many insults Akechi was forced to endure from Oda. Others say Mitsuhide betrayed Nobunaga when Mitsuhide heard a rumor stating that when Japan was unified, Nobunaga was going to transfer all of Mitsuhide's holdings to Nobunaga's page, Ranmaru Mori, with whom Nobunaga was alleged to have been in a ritualized homosexual relationship, a form of patronage known as shudō. No one knows for certain what happened on June 21, 1582 at the Temple at Honnoji.

Another event would come to be questioned that historians cannot agree on to this day; who actually set the temple on fire? Some say it was Mitsuhide's archers, because Mitsuhide was too much of a coward to cross blades with Nobunaga. Others say Nobunaga realized that fighting was futile, so he ordered Ranmaru to burn the temple down around them so no one would be able to claim Nobunaga's head. Despite all the theories regarding his death, one thing is certain…when Mitsuhide gained entry to the remains of the temple, Nobunaga's body could not be found. The bodies of his page, Ranmaru, and his bodyguards that had accompanied Nobunaga to the temple were also missing, along with their weapons.

When news of Nobunaga's death reached the final stretch of resistance to the unification of Japan, the rebels celebrated and drank merrily, believing the war to be over. They drank so much that when a small group of Nobunaga's forces attacked in the dead of night, the rebels were too inebriated to even draw their weapons, and the war ended without any further bloodshed. This was the one thing Nobunaga wanted above all else, so in "Death" he got his final wish.

To this day there is still a great deal of controversy and mystery surrounding Nobunaga's death. I personally believe he faked his death so he could end the war, and also because he wanted to live in peace in the lands he had fought so hard to unify. He wouldn't be able to do that if he lived, so faking his death and dealing with the last shred of resistance was the only way he could accomplish all of his goals. If my theory is correct—and it is entirely plausible, as many of the structures in that time period were constructed with escape routes in the event of a siege, exactly as happened on that day—Nobunaga was a master of strategy, both in politics and on the field of battle. So planning everything from being in that exact temple on that day, when all of his troops save Mitsuhide's were gone, having a small force of his troops in position over the last bit of resistance, being betrayed by Mitsuhide, then "dying," were well within his mental and political abilities. I would almost go so far as to say that Nobunaga deliberately pushed Mitsuhide so Nobunaga could make sure that when the time came, all would go according to plan. If this was true, it would make him the most highly skilled warlord there ever was, and hence the legend he still is to this day.

My story is a loose interpretation of what happened that day and maybe one of many things that could have happened. So please read and enjoy.

Chapter One:
The Brotherhood

Tokyo at night was like a beautiful glittering jewel, so bright it could be seen from the heavens. Modern day Tokyo was different from the time of ancient Japan, when the warlord Nobunaga Oda and his allies, Ieyasu Tokugawa and Hideyoshi Toyotomi, ravaged the land. Now the modern warlords plundered the beauty of Japan and enslaved its people. The aspiring warlord, the rickshaw man, and even the men with no hopes, no dreams; all looked like ants from the top of the skyscraper. "Japan's beauty still astounds me, no matter how many times I see it," a man spoke as he looked around.

There were three, all dressed like ninja straight from the legends. The man who spoke was dressed in a navy blue shinobi shozoku; his forest green eyes took in everything as he walked along the edge of the skyscraper.

"Yes, but nothing quite defeats the beauty of an enemy lying dead before you, his blood pooling at your feet as the beautiful red substance cools on your fingers." This man wore a black shinobi shozoku with black plates of armor covering his stomach and chest. His red eyes were focused on the sky as thunder rumbled around them.

"Silence your destructive thoughts, Takeo. We have a mission tonight, and I will not have you jeopardize it with unnecessary bloodshed. Makoto, get away from the edge."

Makoto hopped down, his grin hidden by the cowl on his face. "You need to learn to relax, Ryu."

Ryu's lightning blue eyes glared at his brethren from where he balanced atop the tower's antenna. They were not related by blood, but by life experiences, a bond arguably stronger than blood. Ryu's navy blue shinobi shozoku didn't make a sound as he jumped off his perch; all three wore swords of different styles. Ryu's sword was thirty-two inches long, resting diagonally across his back, the hilt proudly displayed over his shoulder, wrapped in black leather. Takeo wore a tanto twenty inches long across the back of his waist, the hilt just within reach of his right hand, wrapped with deep red leather. Makoto wore his sword like Takeo's, but drew it like a normal katana, the hilt wrapped in dark green leather.

"When do we begin?" Takeo looked at Ryu, his hand twitching toward his sword.

Ryu glanced at Takeo before closing his eyes. "At the first strike of lightning."

Takeo sighed, but nodded as he stared at the sky again, silently hoping for lightning.

Ryu looked ahead as a ripple went through him, and his eyes shot open. This was the moment he had been waiting for, and without a word he ran towards the ledge and vaulted over it, the wind whistling in his ears as he plummeted toward the ground. A second later he saw a flash of lightning and gave in to his instincts, and heard a ripping sound as black leathery wings burst from his back. Slowing his descent, he flipped and gently landed on a railing outside an apartment next to a river. Within seconds Takeo landed on Ryu's right, his brown leathery wings folding behind him, his eyes alight with dark intent. The railing jostled as Makoto landed on his left, a pair of white avian-like wings folding on his back, while Ryu's folded around him, hiding his body, and more importantly, his right hand from view, the skin having blackened, red veins pulsing with a demonic aura.

Takeo sighed. "Kami-sama (Kami: A Divine being in Shinto Religion) I love being me. I get such a rush when my wings come out."

Ryu shook his head as movement caught his eyes. "You two go ahead. Remember, enter through the roof and don't be seen." Two sets of eyes turned to him.

"I thought we were all supposed to enter and carry out the mission; that's why we waited for the storm, right?" Makoto cocked his head at Ryu.

Ryu turned to Makoto. "We waited for the storm so that way we make less noise on entry, but I forgot something, so you two go ahead and I'll catch up."

Takeo nodded, a maniacal glint in his eyes, and took off into the sky. Makoto looked at Ryu before he flew after his over eager companion. As soon as they were out of eye sight Ryu bunched up his leg muscles and leapt into the air, landing on the roof of the apartment building. He turned around and was greeted with the sight of fifty enemy ninja, all with swords drawn.

Ryu chuckled as his wings unfolded, revealing his demonic hand. Some of the ninja backed away from him, and he saw a red rose on the backs of their white shinobi shozoku. "The Tokugawa clan...I thought you bastards had learned by now not to mess with us, and yet, here you are."

A man in the front spoke. "Our leader wishes you dead."

Ryu growled. "Old man Tokugawa sent you to kill me, but he only sends a handful? He must be going senile."

The man spoke again. "No, we have a new leader now, and Master Akuma has made us stronger."

Ryu glared; a change within the Tokugawa clan was not good news. Without wasting any more words, Ryu closed his eyes as he reached for the hilt of his sword with his demonic hand and drew it with practiced ease. His eyes snapped open and he charged forward. He crossed the expanse between him and his enemies in a few short strides and brought his sword down in a vertical slash, splitting the one who had spoken from shoulder to waist. Lightning flashed, and he cut through another enemy, severing his head, and a fountain of blood poured from the body. Ryu cut through them one by one, severing arms and legs from his opponents. Thunder rumbled and it started pouring rain, mixing with the blood and washing it away, leaving behind only body parts. Ryu flashed around the rooftop, killing anything that got in his way.

Swords bit into his body, leaving shallow cuts as shuriken flashed by his ears, and by the next peal of lightning only two people stood on the roof. Ryu was covered in blood, most of it belonging to the bodies around him. His sword was in his left hand, impaled on a body, and his demonic hand was around the last enemy's throat, but a sword was sticking out of his stomach.

He stared down at it before looking into the surprised eyes of his prey. "Ouch, that hurts." He growled as he snapped the Tokugawa's neck, the sword slipping out of him as the corpse fell to the ground to join his severed allies' remains, the only whole body left amongst a small attack force. Ryu panted as the hole in his gut hissed before closing, and looked down at the tattered remains of his shirt. He scoffed as he ripped it off and cast it away, his sword dripping blood and water. A splash behind him made him whirl around. Standing ten feet in front of him was a man twice his size, a sword with a crimson hilt clutched in his right hand, his body covered with the red armor of a samurai.

Ryu growled as his hand pulsed. "You must be Akuma."

The man inclined his head. "I am Akuma Tokugawa. I lead my clan with honor against the scourge that is Oda, with my father's passing. You, Ryu Oda, must die."

Ryu scoffed as he slung the blade of his sword across his shoulder. "Is that so?" He kicked a head from one of the corpses at Akuma. It bounced off his armor like one of the many raindrops falling from the heavens. Ryu's eyes narrowed as he charged at the hulking Akuma. With no trace of fear or hesitation as their swords met, the sound was lost in the howl of the rain and the crash of thunder.

***

Makoto and Takeo winged their way around buildings, the occasional strike of lightning all that illuminated their way. As they flew, Makoto had an uneasy twinge in his stomach. "Takeo, do you think Ryu is all right?"

Takeo scoffed as they flew, his eyes set forward, their target his only objective. "I'm sure he's fine; it'll take more than a few enemies to beat him."

Makoto stopped as he looked back. "Did you say enemies?"

Takeo stopped and glared at him. "You didn't see the enemies on the roof of that apartment? You're slipping."

Makoto glared. "How could you leave him? He might need us!"

Takeo shook his head. "No, you know what he would say; 'the mission is always the first priority.' So let's go."

Makoto didn't move. "No, 'the mission is always the first priority, *after* your allies are safe.' We are breaking his rule by not helping him."

Takeo growled, but the sound was lost to the wind. "He made the rule, and when he told us to go ahead, he broke the rules. So now until we get home the rules don't matter. If you're so worried then go back, but I'm finishing the mission." He turned around and flew faster than before, leaving Makoto looking at his back. Makoto hesitated for two seconds before he shot back in the direction of Ryu.

***

Takeo landed on the rooftop of the building where the mission was to take place; he looked over his shoulder and found no one had followed. *Fine, fuck them. I'll do it myself.* He approached the rooftop entrance with a gleeful grin under his cowl…the mission was supposed to be dangerous and fraught with bad guys. Well, they were someone's bad guys. He steadied his breathing as his hand closed around the handle and turned it; it was locked. He braced himself and in one smooth motion, pulled the door from its hinges just as a crack of thunder boomed around him.

Flawless infiltration. He descended the stairs just as it started to rain outside, moving with caution, his hand resting on his sword. His barely perceivable breathing was the only sound as he reached the bottom. He felt his internal alarms going off, as no one was guarding the doors. None of them.

His instincts were telling him to leave, but as he turned, a scent caught his attention; something he felt he should know, but the answer was dancing at the edge of his consciousness and wouldn't let him depart before he had investigated it. He followed the scent down stairs and around corners until at last he came to the source, at the exact place the mission was to be carried out. He opened the door and was hit with the source of the smell, one he could finally place…the scent of a fresh kill.

He approached the body sitting in front of the desk in an executive's chair and snorted. "Mission accomplished." Someone had carried out their assassination mission for them, but the assassin had done a sloppy job, as the head was crushed on itself as if hit with a large, heavy blunt object. Takeo studied the damage and his eyes widened. He leapt over the desk just as the roof caved in around the body and a large figure dropped into the room from the opening.

The dust cleared and Takeo got an unobscured view of the assassin. His chest spanned two feet across and was covered with an open white gi top, revealing his chiseled chest and ripped stomach that looked like it could take a direct hit from a car and the car would regret it. Baggy green gi pants covered his legs, and on his feet he wore black tabi shoes. He looked at Takeo with red eyes and a grin on his face that made Takeo's blood boil and his hand clench around the hilt of his blade. The man's red hair was spiked, and judging by the smell, it wasn't with hair gel. Takeo slowly unsheathed his blade as the figure stood with his back straight. He was at least two heads taller than Takeo, and carried himself with an air of absolute power. He breathed slowly as the two fighters looked at each other, one with an amused grin on his face and the other with a glare that would kill a lesser man.

The man slung a great sword over his shoulder as he spoke. "Hey bro."

***

Makoto flew as fast as he could back to Ryu. He didn't know how, but something deep inside of him knew Ryu was in danger. As he flew he suddenly cried out and fell, holding his stomach as it started to bleed like a wound had been inflicted on him. A sudden updraft kept him from hitting a rooftop at speeds that would've killed him, but even as he grew accustomed to the pain it vanished, along with any trace that it was ever there.

Before he could think about it, his senses kicked in and he dropped from the sky as a sword flew over his head. With a few powerful beats of his wings, he was on level ground with his attacker, and his eyes widened as his attacker looked at him with forest green eyes and a calm expression on his face. One side was hidden by bandages, but they didn't cover his hair, which was short, wavy, and the same color as his eyes. A white shirt that didn't seem to get wet and pants that matched the shirt covered his lean body; they also seemed water-proof. On his feet was a pair of plain white sandals. He regarded Makoto with the same calm expression as he raised an elegant rapier in front of him and angel-like wings kept him aloft. "It's been awhile, runt."

***

Ryu growled as yet another of his attacks was blocked and then viciously countered; it was all he could do to block against the vicious monster before him. Akuma was a force

15

to be reckoned with. He blocked everything thrown at him, then countered without mercy. Akuma's armor was scratched from the few times Ryu's attacks could get through, but for every scratch on Akuma's armor, Ryu had two wounds to show for it. He was slowly losing, and the only thing he could think of was a long shot at best, but it seemed to be his only option. He sheathed his blade.

Akuma raised an eyebrow at this as Ryu's stance relaxed. "Ha-ha, so you're finally giving up. I must admit, I was expecting more from you, with all of the stories of your battle prowess."

Ryu ignored him as he raised his hand to the sky; lightning flashed overhead as he closed his eyes, and Akuma's attention shifted to a man that had appeared out of nowhere twenty feet behind Ryu.

Akuma watched the new arrival intently. He radiated malice that would make a dragon flee...he, himself, was tempted to run. He was so intrigued by the man before him that he couldn't take his eyes off him, even as he felt a ripple of power come from his enemy. The dark angel in the sky was calm and his faded blue eyes alight with amusement, as if watching the boy struggle was entertainment for him. But Akuma knew the man was dangerous, perhaps even evil.

His hair was black, as were his clothes, but his shirt was decorated with three silver buckles designed to hold it closed...one over the heart, the next in the middle of his stomach, and the last was peeking out of his pants. The shirt itself was sleeveless, showing arms that sported wired muscle. Whereas the shirt was custom, the pants were plain black gi bottoms. His black spiked hair seemed unaffected by the rain, as were his black tabi shoes.

After his observation, Akuma's gaze shifted back to Ryu, and what he saw set him on edge. Black wings now protruded from his back; his eyes were fixed on Akuma, and they too had changed. They were now pure black, with a single point of red the size of a dime right in the middle.

Ryu's raised hand had cracked and was now pulsing with a black aura around it, and seemed to crackle with power. The lightning had increased to the point that the sky was almost constantly alight with flash after flash.

After a few seconds, just as Akuma decided to stop Ryu from completing whatever he was doing, a single bolt came down, no bigger than a katana blade, and struck Ryu's hand in the center of his palm, encasing his hand with power; power forged from raw lightning.

Ryu closed his hand and everything stopped. The rain was gone and the clouds dissipated. He opened his hand, and Akuma could see that the power was still there, enveloping Ryu's forearm to form a kind of blade.

Ryu was panting as if he were holding the power back by sheer force of will. "Rai Ken!" (Lightning sword)

He held the blade of electricity parallel with his body, but the power looked barely focused. Small bolts danced up and down his arm, cutting open flesh, but his eyes never left Akuma's, never betrayed the pain he must have felt. He ran forward the first few steps and Akuma readied himself to deflect the attack, but suddenly Ryu disappeared. Akuma looked around, but Ryu was nowhere to be found.

Unexpectedly, Akuma was thrown backwards, his armor dented inward. His heels connected with the ledge, threatening to throw him over. As soon as he regained his balance, he saw Ryu standing where Akuma had been a second ago. *How? How did he become so fast?* He looked incredulously at the boy then at the dent in his armor; while the attack hadn't pierced it, it had severely dented his best armor.

The dark angel shook his head and made himself known. "You call that an attack? Allow me to show you how it's done."

He raised his hand as Ryu's head snapped to him with a dark glare in his eyes. Akuma quickly thought of a way to stop him, but he wasn't given a fraction of the time he'd had with Ryu. A second later, the attack formed in his hand and condensed into a fine blade on his arm. "Rai Ken." He said the words calmly as he disappeared without having to move.

Akuma was ready to block this time and waited for the attack, but there was a sudden horrible pain in his back and he could only stare at the bloody hand protruding from his chest. The hand withdrew and took a good portion of Akuma with it, and the dark angel floated over his head and landed in front of him. "That's how a master does it, baby brother."

Ryu growled as Akuma fell sideways, dead. "Damn you Mitsuo, you may have superior control over the Rai Ken, but I don't need a petty trick to kill you." Ryu drew his blade and placed both hands on it, with it positioned in front of him.

Mitsuo flicked his hand and splattered fresh gore on the roof before he drew his own plain black katana. "Do your worst."

Ryu growled as he flashed across the rooftop and slashed at his elder. Before the sword could hit home, Mitsuo was gone, leaving the sword to pass through thin air. Ryu whirled around to block a horizontal slash aimed at his back. "Not bad Ryu, but not good enough," came the mocking tone, followed by the bite of a blade across his undefended front.

Mitsuo was everywhere at once, yet as soon as Ryu turned he was gone and the sword bit into Ryu's body again. He was littered with shallow wounds within moments, as what should have been a vicious fight was reduced to a slaughter. He had no way to defend himself as the world swirled and he hit the roof, too tired to move. His sword slipped from his grasp as he heard footsteps moving toward his head. "Tut, tut. You're supposed to be all powerful, and you can't even cross swords with me for ten seconds before you're on the ground bleeding. It's disappointing that this is all you have to offer."

His brother bent down, his sword sheathed, and a look

of disappointment in his eyes; a look that Ryu had hated growing up. He shut his eyes to escape the gaze and Mitsuo shook his head. "You were always so…*weak.*"

Ryu's eyes shot open. "I'm not weak!" He growled as he raised his head, glaring at Mitsuo.

Mitsuo scoffed. "Then rise…rise and fight. Or, lie down and die." Something in Ryu cracked as his hand pulsed erratically, his eyes bled to black, and a small ember roared to life right in the middle of them again.

"I'M NOT WEAK!" Mitsuo turned toward him with a shocked look on his face at the demonic edge to Ryu's voice. Ryu flashed, sword in hand, and Mitsuo barely had time to guard against the slash that sent him skidding back, a grin clear on his face.

"There's the monster I came to see." Mitsuo flashed to him, and they engaged in combat that could be heard for miles around as thunder and lightning flashed overhead. They danced for what seemed like hours, but only minutes went by as they clashed, flew apart, and clashed again. The rain had started again as Ryu attempted to gain the upper hand, but nothing he did worked. His hand was pulsing slower and slower until it stopped and he was himself again. Mitsuo scoffed as Ryu's attacks lost their ferocity, their intent to kill.

Mitsuo slashed and Ryu flew back to the edge, his breaths coming in small gasps as Mitsuo approached him, a grin on his face. Ryu tried to stand but his legs wouldn't support him. Mitsuo came to stand in front of him and slapped away his halfhearted slash. "You're almost ready to fight me…almost."

He kneed Ryu in the face and sent him over into the waters below. Ryu fell the fifty feet while staring at his brother, who looked down at him, his face set in stone. Ryu flipped over and over, catching sight of the town, sounds of cars and people, then Mitsuo. Ryu blinked as he hit the water and was submerged in darkness.

***

Takeo growled at the man before him as the giant moved his blade in front of his body. "Nori, you bastard!" The giant, Nori, feigned hurt.

"After all this time, that's all you have to say to me? I'm hurt little brother…deeply hurt. Well, I'll just have to make you hurt worse, won't I?" He leapt forward, bringing his blade down, and Takeo jumped away at the last moment, letting the sword pass by him and go through the floor. Nori dashed at Takeo again, this time with a diagonal slash that Takeo *just* had time to dodge under. He barely had enough time to retaliate, slashing a red line into his brother's chest, before he had to dodge again. Nori looked down at the wound and smirked.

"Now you're in trouble." Faster than a six foot sword should be able to move, he slashed at Takeo again and again, never letting up as Takeo bounced and dodged everything, not getting another chance to strike. Finally, with a grin on his face, Nori pulled back his sword and slammed it into the ground next to him, one hand on the hilt while the other wiped his brow.

"Phew! You're bouncier then I remember; just hold still so I can cleave you in half already."

Takeo grinned as he flashed and buried his sword to the hilt in Nori's abdomen. The giant's grin faded, replaced with a scowl.

"Now I'm pissed." He let go of his sword and his huge fists burst into flame as he slammed them into Takeo's gut, lifting him off the ground and forcing him to relinquish his blade, not stopping the assault. He slammed his fist into Takeo's gut again, sending him flying and imbedding him in the wall. Nori pulled the blade from his body before throwing it at Takeo like a spear, and watched as it pierced Takeo's charred flesh and nailed him to the wall.

Takeo looked at his own sword for a few seconds before trying to pull it out, stopping when the act only caused a lance of agony to race through him. He looked at Nori, who extinguished his fists. The giant approached with a cocky stride and his sword in his hand, and smirked as he stood over Takeo.

"Hah; you were all right, but you still fight with your anger. Until you overcome that, you'll only ever be adequate." Nori turned around and walked away as Takeo struggled with his sword. Just as Nori reached the edge of the hole he'd knocked in the floor, Takeo growled.

"No matter where you run, no matter how well you hide, I'll track you down and kill you. I swear to Kami-sama himself, I'll kill you if it's the last thing I do. I'll kill you!"

Nori flashed a grin over his shoulder. "I hope one day you can make good on that, hatchling." And with that he was gone, and Takeo was left with a thousand questions and one painful problem. He looked at the blade before he closed his eyes, grasped the hilt with both hands, and with one vicious tug ripped it from his body. He looked at the blade in his hand with a grimace. The hot rage bubbled in his chest like liquid fire as his mind carried him eight years into the past, to memories better left forgotten.

***

A ten-year-old Takeo grinned as he slipped out of his bedroom window into the night beyond. It was another night that he decided to disobey his parents, both of whom were trying to groom him to accept his role as one of the Chosen. But he blatantly refused to fit into the box that they had carved for him. Takeo swore to himself he would be just like his older brother Nori, who was wild and untamed. The first step was to disobey his parents at every turn.

Takeo's feet hit the ground and he was off, running through an old style village, down streets that he knew well enough to navigate in any weather. He felt the same sense of euphoria that he always did. The life he was leading was free and blissful, he was happy, and that was all that mattered. But he had no idea that while his life was free, it didn't mean

21

somebody wouldn't attempt to take his freedom from him.

He was suddenly surrounded by six men, all wearing hoods to cover their faces. The one at the front, the apparent leader, drew a sword and slung it over his shoulder.

"Well, well. What have we here boys? I see an able bodied boy who's perfect for labor." Takeo looked around, fear the last thing on his mind. To him he was invincible, untouchable. He fell into a battle stance and the men jeered.

"Oh no, boys, this one intends to fight." The leader threw back his hood and Takeo got a good look at him. With his short brown, cropped hair and lack of distinguishing marks, he could easily blend into a crowd and vanish if he was asked. A smirk was firmly planted on his face, but it quickly fled, and was replaced with a look of pure terror. Takeo's grin widened before he saw that the man's gaze wasn't directed at him, but at something over his shoulder.

Takeo turned around and found the source of their fear. Instead of an army or even ten men, it was one single, solitary man...Nori Toyotomi, with a massive sword slung on his back. "Why are you bothering my little bro?" It wasn't a question...it was a warning. Quick as they had come the men were gone, vanished into the night. Takeo turned to Nori, a glare in his eyes.

"I could've handled them." He stomped his foot in rage and Nori chuckled; even at nineteen he was huge. Thick arms were attached to a broad barrel chest that led down to large, thick tree trunk like legs. His trademark grin was firmly in place, and thick unruly hair flared wildly on his head.

"I know, but still it's nice to say a few words and then watch the dust clouds they kick up as they run." Takeo growled but let it go as Nori laid a massive hand on his head.

"Don't worry little bro. One day, before you even realize it, you'll command more fear and respect than even me...well, one day when I'm not around to hog it all. Ha-ha." Nori laughed as he led Takeo back home.

Two months after the incident in the village Takeo awoke to the sounds of fighting. He jumped out of his bed and grabbed his father's old katana off the wall as he ran out the door. The sounds were coming from the center of the village, and as he ran toward the source of the sound, all at once it died. A second later Nori appeared beside him, his grin firmly in place. Takeo stopped and looked at his brother. Nori was covered from head to toe in blood, and had more than his share of wounds littering his body.

"What's happened, Nori?" Nori looked at Takeo before he shook his head.

"I can't believe it, you of all people. Why you?" There was a remorseful tone mixed with the wicked glee he seemed to feel. Takeo took a step back at the look in Nori's eyes.

"Me what? Nori, I don't understand."

Nori shook his head as he looked at the sky. "No, I don't suppose you do. Why would you, after all? It's not like Mother or Father told you anything. Oh well." Takeo barely dodged a vertical slash as Nori impaled his sword in the ground, in the spot where Takeo had been half a second earlier.

"What the hell are you doing?"

Nori grinned as he wrenched his blade from the ground. "Removing an obstacle. Now quit moving and make this easy for me." Nori slashed at him again, this time with a horizontal slash that Takeo barely dodged. Nori lost his grip on his sword and it went flying into a building as Nori fell to the ground, holding his chest.

"Not now, I'm so close! Ahhh!" A blood red orb pulled itself free from his back and slammed into Takeo's chest, sending him flying into a fruit stand. Takeo's world slowly turned black.

He watched as Nori fell into the dirt, and a single tear tracked down Takeo's face. "Why Nori?"

***

23

Takeo stabbed the blade into the ground next to him, and watched as blood slowly seeped from the wound. He chuckled. "What a way to die." He thought he heard chuckling but dismissed it, until a voice spoke.

"You're not gonna die. Ryu would never let me hear the end of it."

Takeo's head shot to look at a man wearing a loose fitting gi shirt that wasn't properly tied and showed half his chest, along with a pair of loose, faded gi pants and plain wooden sandals. He was silent as he walked toward Takeo. "Mamoru-sensei? What are you doing here?" His sensei tipped his bamboo wicker hat back to smile at his student, his blue eyes dancing with mirth despite the situation.

"Saving you, apparently." Takeo grunted as Mamoru lifted him off the ground and led him back the way Takeo had come in.

"Sensei, where are the others?"

***

Makoto panted as his brother attacked and danced away, never getting close enough for a counterattack. They had dropped to a rooftop, the same Makoto had almost had a forced meeting with earlier. He knew Ryu was in trouble, but there was nothing he could do about it. "Please, Takeshi. Ryu's in trouble."

Takeshi smiled as he flicked his rapier. "Oh, by now I'm sure Mitsuo is taking care of him." Makoto felt his heart flutter as he remembered the last time Ryu had fought Mitsuo. He tried to take off, but was slammed into the ground by a gust of wind; he glared at Takeshi, the source of the attack.

Makoto stood up, knowing there was no way he was getting out of there without a fight; he drew his sword and fell into a battle stance.

"Finally, you're getting serious."

Makoto flew at Takeshi and slashed at him, only for him to disappear and reappear behind him.

24

"I'm not playing with you, runt." Makoto blinked at the same words spoken so long ago.

***

Eight-year-old Makoto threw himself into his attack as he slashed at Takeshi with his Bokken. But Takeshi merely side stepped him and whacked him on the back of his legs. "Wrong, little runt. You need to be more graceful if you're going to take my place. The others will protect you while you cover them. Never throw yourself into an attack; you leave yourself open for a counter attack."

Makoto was on his feet before he lunged again, and this time Takeshi hit him hard enough to throw him through the air. "I am your enemy Makoto, not your brother. Fight me like I'll kill you."

Makoto was on his feet as he glared at Takeshi. "You're not helping and you're not even giving me a chance to win."

Takeshi appeared in front of him and drove his knee into Makoto's sternum. "I'm not playing with you, runt."

***

Years later and Takeshi still saw him as a child, a "runt," not the warrior he knew himself to be…the warrior he had groomed himself to be. Makoto attacked, his moves fluent and graceful but filled with anger, and still Takeshi was able to block everything while barely moving.

Takeshi shook his head as he disappeared. Makoto dropped his sword as he felt a pinch at the base of his neck before he went numb. He fell forward onto Takeshi's sword, and it pierced through his heart. "You're not worth leaving alive." Takeshi pulled out his sword and was gone before Makoto hit the roof, his world slowly fading to black as his mind drifted to memories of a time when he revered his brother.

***

Seven-year-old Makoto sniffled as his brother led him by the hand to his new home. His parents had just died, taken in a horrible raid, and now he had to live with his

25

grandmother, a woman he hardly knew. The only thing that kept him going was Takeshi, who was always calm; nothing could faze him; he never showed any real emotions, just varying degrees of calm. Takeshi knocked and Makoto hid behind his brother as Takeshi spoke with an old woman.

Takeshi moved to the side and gently urged Makoto to come forward. The woman was old, even Makoto could tell that. She had short gray hair and her skin was marked by wrinkles, but her smile was welcoming, and despite the obvious effort, she lowered herself down to Makoto's height and held out one of her aged hands.

"Hello little one, my name is Chiyo. But you can call me Granny, like everyone else." Makoto didn't move at first. Then slowly, he reached out and took her hand, and she pulled him closer before embracing him.

"Granny's going to take care of you now." Makoto sniffled before he started crying, and Chiyo immediately started soothing him. Before long Makoto calmed down, and she led them inside to the place that would be their home for the next three years.

The years passed quickly and were filled with happiness and laughter. Then one day, when Makoto and Takeshi returned home from the market with some food, they walked through the front door with Makoto calling out that they were home. When they didn't get an answer they began to get worried. Makoto ran into the kitchen and found his grandmother on the floor. He tried shaking her but she wouldn't wake up.

Takeshi came at his call before vanishing out the front door and returning within seconds with help. They went to the hospital, and half an hour later the nurses placed a white sheet over Granny in her bed. Makoto cried into Takeshi's chest while Takeshi talked to the doctor and learned that the woman had passed away due to old age. The doctor assured them that it was painless, and by the end of the week, they had attended their grandmother's funeral.

Takeshi began to withdraw from Makoto more and more, and after two months, while Makoto was in the woods, his world was changed forever.

Makoto was walking home from training in the woods, and came upon a sight he never wanted to see. He had just left the tree line when he felt something was very wrong, so he hurriedly took a shortcut through the woods. He stopped and looked over a barren landscape where his village should be, but it was gone.

"What…what happened?" He heard a sound behind him and found Takeshi leaning against a tree.

"Don't worry about what happened; the village annoyed me so I wiped it from existence."

Makoto shook his head as he looked at Takeshi, who was picture perfect calm. "What?"

Takeshi picked up a rock, and with a small sigh held it up for Makoto to see. Then he placed it on the ground and held his hand over it. With hardly any energy from Takeshi, the wind whipped out and crushed the rock.

"Imagine that on a village wide scale. Believe me, it was quite painless." Takeshi vanished and Makoto felt a pair of arms drape themselves over his shoulders as a voice spoke into his ear.

"And now I'll do the same thing to you."

Makoto stumbled away and looked at Takeshi with shock. "Why? What did I do?"

Takeshi chuckled as a small ball of wind formed in his hand. "It's not what you did, it's what you were going to do. The village was going to take my power and give it to you, so I killed them. Now, I'll deal with you and keep my power until I decide to relinquish control of it." The ball lifted from his hand and flew over Makoto's head before rapidly expanding.

"Any last words, runt?" Makoto stared at the wind gale in horror before suddenly it was gone, and Takeshi was lying on the ground clutching his chest. He gazed at Makoto with

27

a stone cold look as a green ball rose from his back and slammed into Makoto, sending him flying through the trees, where he slammed his back into a tree and was rendered unconscious before his body hit the ground.

***

Makoto drifted back to the present to hear a voice he knew so well.

"Damn. He's getting serious." His vision winked out as his sensei carried him to safety.

***

Ryu hit the cold water. He didn't kick or move, he just sunk to the bottom. He didn't breathe, but his insides were in turmoil. *I lost. Again. I can't beat him no matter how many times we fight. I can't win. Years of training for nothing. Why the hell is he always stronger?*

His air was running out, his body was numb, but his mind kept circling the same questions. What was that power he felt? Why was Mitsuo always stronger? Did he have too much of a head start, or was he just not ascending fast enough? If that was the case, how could he ascend faster? Did he need a new sensei? Was his holding him back? Were the other two holding him back? He opened his mouth and screamed; too many questions and no answers. His air was gone, he was surrounded by water, but suddenly he could breathe. He opened his eyes and inhaled violently as he found himself in a boat...the boatman, the same person he had just been thinking about. "Sensei?" His voice was raspy and the rain wasn't helping his voice carry, but his sensei still nodded.

"Yo! Having a bad day?" Mamoru waved lightly as he rowed the boat towards shore.

Ryu shook his head with a snort as the rain thinned. "Not at all; I enjoy knocking on Death's door, then running. It's fun."

Mamoru chuckled as he looked Ryu over. He was covered in cuts and was shirtless, but he appeared to be in decent health. "Yes, I hear he hates that. But Ryu, you have to be more careful. You and the others may be eighteen, but I worry sometimes that you're pushing too hard."

Ryu let his head fall back as he ripped off his cowl and glared at the sky. His short, dark blue hair was spiked from the water as he sighed. Mamoru cocked his head. "Speak if you need to."

Ryu growled. "Alright; I want to know why he is so much stronger than me. Have I not killed enough? Have I not put enough of my blood, sweat, and tears into my training? Is there something he was taught that I wasn't? What am I missing? I am supposed to be the Lord of Lightning, and yet I can't beat him. Or wannabe Lord?" Ryu didn't raise his head, instead choosing to aim his questions at the sky.

Mamoru raised an eyebrow at the "Wannabe Lord" comment, but chose to let it go for now. "No Ryu, I've taught you everything I can at this stage. You know we can't proceed until you complete the Bond."

Ryu rolled his shoulders and shifted, but still didn't lift his head. "Then I'll train on my own."

Mamoru sighed as he angled the boat back to sea, anticipating a long talk. "Still adamant about that?"

Ryu glared at the sky, but nodded. "I will not do as the Elders ask, not in this. You know that as well as I. I'm not some puppet they can command. I'll follow their orders in respect for the chain of command, but when it comes to my personal life they can all eat a dick."

Mamoru laughed at this, but as soon as he regained his breath he sighed. "Ryu, you can't keep denying it. Eventually you'll succumb. You do know this, right?"

Ryu shut his eyes with a sigh. "I know, but I will fight for as long as possible. Maybe Mitsuo will finish it one of these days and I'll never have to worry."

Mamoru shook his head sadly. "Come now, Ryu, the Elders knew what they were doing when they made the pact.

It's not their fault the gods' gift carried such a price with it."

Ryu's fist slammed through the bottom of the boat as his head snapped to glare at Mamoru, but the water didn't flow in, kept at bay by a shift of Mamoru's hand.

"Gift? *Gift*? It's a fucking curse if I've ever heard of one. I will not follow it just to please those old bastards, who don't even know what side of their weapons cut anymore. The best I can do is *tolerate* Makoto. I will not become intimate with him just to appease this curse. I would sooner rip my heart out and bleed it over an open fire." With that Ryu let his head fall back, before continuing in a softer tone. "Takeo can have him. They're a match made in hell as far as I'm concerned."

Mamoru nodded as he directed the boat back to shore, as Ryu's thoughts wandered to the words his sensei spoke to him when he was eleven—when his sensei had first told him of his destiny. *"Ryu, there are three stages to your training. First, we train you in Taijutsu, hand-to-hand combat. Then, we train you in Kenjutsu, sword fighting. Then the final part has a condition you must fulfill. You have to have a bond stronger than brotherhood with Makoto."* Ryu closed his eyes.

"Wind will desire Lightning, Fire will desire Wind, and Lightning will bond with Wind. In this, the Bond will be complete and Lightning will create Fire, Wind will fan Fire. And Fire will lend his power to both."

Ryu chuckled even as he shook his head; something wasn't right. He could feel it, almost taste it, then his head shot forward again. "The mission!"

Mamoru held up his right hand. "Easy Ryu. The mission was a success. The Council won't complain how it got done as long as the leak was closed."

Ryu's eyes narrowed and Mamoru sighed. "From what Takeo said, Nori killed the informant."

Ryu stiffened. "Nori? That means Takeshi...Makoto. Takeo. How are they?"

Mamoru rubbed the back of his head. "Takeo's recovering from semi-fatal wounds; it's Makoto I'm worried about."

Ryu shot to his feet and was in the air before Mamoru could take a breath. Mamoru shook his head. "Oh dear, he never does stop to listen." Mamoru dissolved into water, and the boat sank. Gone like its passengers.

***

Ryu crashed into his sensei's Zen garden and ran toward his sensei's home; a small traditional Japanese home located on an island in the middle of the sea, far from the city; normally a thirty-minute flight, but Ryu had done it in ten. He pushed open the door and was welcomed by the sight of the place he and his team had called home for the last ten years, ever since their lives had been irreversibly altered at the tender age of eight.

Ryu stalked across the room from the front door as he kicked off his tabi shoes and walked toward Makoto's room, through the living room where there were six sitting mats and a couch for Takeo, since he refused to sit on the floor. Ryu shot a glance at the counter where his sensei would usually sit and drink tea, while they talked about anything and everything. Six stools, three on the living room side and three on the kitchen side, where they would eat and talk about what had happened to them through the extent of the day. Ryu directed his gaze to Makoto's door before he threw it open to find his brothers in the room. Takeo was wearing a pair of gray sweat pants, and was wrapped in bandages. Makoto was also wearing gray sweats, but didn't have more than cuts and bruises on him. Ryu growled when his eyes met the bandage over Makoto's heart. "Damage report."

Takeo looked at him with sad red eyes from Makoto's bedside, his short dark red hair caked with blood. "Nothing I can't recover from. Makoto though...." He shrugged his shoulders. "Ryu, Takeshi stabbed him through the heart; he's been unconscious since Mamoru-sensei brought him in."

Ryu growled. "That bastard!"

Ryu walked across the room and Takeo stepped away from the bed to lean against a corner, as Ryu knelt next to the bed and gently touched Makoto's deep green hair. Ryu grimaced as he shifted the bandages and a small trickle of blood slipped down Makoto's chest.

"Sensei said there's nothing we can do. He was gonna consult the Elders and ask for help as soon as he was done helping you. I think that's where he is right now. I'm afraid he'll bleed out before they can intervene, though."

Ryu growled again. *I could let it go. I don't have to do this; the Elders will come up with a solution in time. They always do. But if they don't, this could move beyond what I have the ability to take.*

Ryu nodded to himself as he looked over his shoulder. "Takeo, stay back while I fix this."

Takeo looked at him before realization donned on him. "Ryu, don't do this. The Elders will help, they have to!" Takeo took a step forward, but it was too late.

Ryu had already reached for his ignored bond and forced life into it. Faster than Takeo could blink, Makoto's wounds had vanished and new wounds appeared on Ryu, and he groaned as his legs started to buckle. A small, perfect knife thin cut appeared over his heart. Takeo grabbed him before he hit the floor and stared into Ryu's pain filled eyes. Takeo shook his head furiously. "Idiot, you should've waited."

Ryu's hand came up and clasped one of Takeo's shoulders. "No time; I had to do something before it could get worse." Ryu stood up after his abrupt fall, pain racking his body. His healing abilities had kept the edge off, but now that they had been exhausted, the pain was coursing throughout his nerves, causing his body to twitch.

"Come on, you stupid bastard, get your ass into bed." Takeo forced Ryu to lean on him as they walked out of the room. As they entered the living room they heard a snort,

Masters of the Skies

and they both looked up to see Mamoru leaning against the wall with a grim look on his face.

"The Elders can't help." Mamoru grimaced as the words left his mouth.

Ryu shook his head as Takeo helped him across the room. "Of course not, they can't do anything. Never have, never will. Doesn't matter, we look out for our own."

Mamoru shook his head, a small smile playing on his mouth. "I figured you would do something stupid."

Ryu shrugged as Takeo led him to the door next to Makoto's. Ryu was about to open the door when his sensei spoke. "I need to talk to you before you retire."

Ryu gritted his teeth before he nodded; he shrugged off Takeo and turned around as Takeo glared at Mamoru. "Sensei, he needs to rest. He's way worse than me and Makoto; I really thi—"

A sharp sound from Ryu stopped him. "Enough Takeo, go. The master wishes to speak, so I'll endure."

Takeo scoffed. "Ryu, I—"

Ryu spun around and glared. "I didn't ask what you think…now leave! That's an order."

Takeo growled, but snapped straight. "Yes sir," and then he was gone, disappearing into the room on the other side of Makoto's.

Only then did Ryu hunch over in pain, his breath coming in small bursts. This only lasted a few seconds before he straightened up and turned to his sensei, who sighed. "Maybe it is better if this waits."

Ryu sat on a stool across from him and shook his head. "No Sensei, we need to talk."

Mamoru nodded as he took off his bamboo hat, placed it on the counter, and ran his right hand through his short sandy blond hair. Mamoru focused his light brown eyes on his student, keeping all the pity he felt from his gaze. "Down to business then. First things first. You posed a lot of questions to me tonight, and I have to ask where they came from. And I'm also forced to ask what you meant when you said, 'Wannabe Lord'?"

Ryu snorted as a dull wash of anger ran through him. "Yeah, you could say righteous anger fueled those questions. As for the wannabe, I meant Akuma Tokugawa, the new and deceased leader of the Tokugawa clan." He shrugged as he looked around the room; it looked like something out of a kung fu movie, complete with a training dummy in the corner. Calligraphy scrolls hung from the walls, each with a meaning to what Mamoru taught. "Death before dishonor" was one that spoke to Ryu the most.

Mamoru nodded sagely. "I had heard that a change in leadership had occurred. I just never thought they would be able to rally that fast. Their grudge against Oda goes back to the beginning. They never could get over the fact that Nobunaga destroyed their castle and killed their people, and I'm sure they will never stop hunting you. You say he's deceased?"

Ryu nodded as he looked back at his sensei, no hint of pain in his eyes. "Yeah, Mitsuo appeared and finished him with a single attack, which brings me to my next set of problems. Mitsuo's so much stronger, and I know it's much more than a five year difference. He knows something that I don't."

Ryu sighed as Mamoru said. "Yes Ryu, he's done more and seen more than you ever will. But he fought through a war, Ryu…an honest to Kami war. That's not something you live through without picking up tricks, which are gone as soon as the war is over. He's also revealed his sword's soul, Ryu. That alone gives him a boost that you'll only be able to catch up with once you do the same."

Ryu growled and glared at Mamoru. "Then tell me how to do that. It seems logical to me."

Mamoru shook his head. "I'm sorry Ryu, it's not that easy. You're not ready. When you're ready it will happen. You will ascend to a new level of power, the likes of which you can't even begin to comprehend. For now, sleep is what you need." With that he stood up and left, leaving Ryu to angrily throw the stool he was sitting on across the room. He watched as it crashed through the front door and smashed against the tree outside. Ryu limped to his door. Sliding it open and slamming it shut only increased his anger, but he sighed irritably and lay down on his bed.

His eyes dully looked around his room. Makoto's and Takeo's rooms were as bare as his, but for a table that his sword rested on. There was a full sized mirror next to the table. Ryu shut his eyes as he felt his sheathe digging into his back, but didn't have the will, or the desire, to remove it. *Maybe sensei's right, I just need to wait, just like I had to wait to unlock my element.*

***

Ryu stood in a forest miles from civilization, watching as a sakura tree bloomed overhead. His sword clutched in both hands in front of him, Mamoru stood across from him with a lazy grip on his blade and a light grin on his face. "Ryu, you're improving fast. But, you still lack your element, and without that you'll never beat your brother."

Ryu growled as his body slowly tensed. "I know that. But you won't tell me how."

Mamoru shook his head. "I can't tell you. You must find the power within you and rip it to the surface. Reach inside yourself, find your center, and rip your power out. Pull every ounce of it to the surface and then, when you have all you can hold, unleash it onto the world. Let your power free, like a beast being tempted with blood finally allowed to rend, tear, and rip through your foes."

Ryu let his sword drop to his side, held in one hand as he relaxed. Trying to fall into himself, he opened his eyes and the garden was gone. He was in a room, a plain brown brick room, and the only light source was a torch hanging on the wall. A door was at the far side of the room, a few shades brighter, but still the same brown.

Ryu started walking towards the door as his footsteps resounded off the walls. "This is my soul." He reached the door, aware that what was on the other side could change him forever, and with one movement he turned the handle and pulled open the door. On the other side was not what he expected...it was a labyrinth of stairs; stairs on the ceiling, on the walls, and doors everywhere. "What is this?"

He heard a cackling that seemed to come from everywhere. "This is you—your soul and your every thought is here." The voice sent chills down his spine, as if it were ice cold and merciless.

"What the hell are you?"

Again he heard the cackle. "Me? I'm everything you are. I'm you and yet I'm not. I am unexplainable. Indefinable. And soon, very soon, I will be unstoppable." Ryu started running, trying to do something. Whether he was running toward the voice or away he didn't know. He just ran as the cackle continued, until he found a pure white door. Without thinking he ran through it and found himself in a room, a lighting blue orb in the middle and a silhouette in the corner that, despite the glowing ball, remained hidden.

All Ryu could see was a pair of acid green eyes and a red vapor that resembled a smirk. "You found me." Ryu growled as he stepped forward, but the figure vanished and Ryu found his feet walking toward the ball.

"What is this?" He reached forward and pulled.

***

Mamoru watched as Ryu became still and his sword dropped. But before it could hit the ground Ryu's eyes snapped open, a lighting blue hue to them as he threw open his arms, electricity erupting from his body, flashing away from him in thousands upon thousands of arcs, each one lashing out in a different direction. Everything around them was destroyed, and Mamoru was forced to leap straight up to avoid the power that leveled every form of life for half a mile. Then, as soon as it came, it was gone and Ryu collapsed. Mamoru landed and was beside him in a second. "That was impressive, unbelievably powerful. Next I will teach you moderation."

Ryu grinned as he closed his eyes, suddenly tired. The last thing he heard before the world faded was Mamoru. "That was stronger than anything I've ever seen. If he could harness that into an attack it would probably kill him, but whoever he was fighting wouldn't have a chance."

***

Ryu snorted. The difference, back then Mitsuo had told him how to fall into himself. This time he had no idea how to awaken his sword, and no one to tell him how. He sighed as he drifted off, hoping for a reprieve.

***

Drenched in sweat and covered in dirt, a ten-year-old Ryu ran through the Oda village, located on Mount Fuji. Men and women dressed in shinobi shozoku flashed by him as he ran at breakneck speeds. Finally, he came upon his home, a two-story complex with a lightning bolt on the front gates, which he leapt over. He raced through the doors, throwing off his sandals as he ran into the dining area and flew into his seat at the end of a large table, with a chair next to him and two chairs across. He looked up as his mother came in, her long, brown braided hair swishing as she walked up to the table with a platter of food in her arms.

"Hello, Mother."

She smiled before frowning. "Ryu, why are you sweaty and dirty?"

He grinned sheepishly. "Sorry Mother, I just got back and didn't have time to clean up."

She giggled as she put the food on the table. "I swear, ten year olds never change." She pointed down the hall and he ran off to clean up. When he came back he was clean, the food was spread out, and both chairs at the head of the table were occupied...one by his mother, the other by a stern looking man. Ryu immediately straightened up and approached them calmly. The man looked at him and Ryu fell into a deep bow.

"Father." His father nodded and Ryu took his seat.

While he was still calmly waiting for his lifeline, his father said, "Your brother will not be joining us tonight."

Ryu's hand shook as he grabbed some food and put it on his plate. "I hope everything's all right." His voice shook as his father's eyes narrowed; his father leaned forward and he shook worse.

"Why are you shaking? Stop showing weakness! You are going to be one of the Three. I'll say it one more time…either find the steel in your spine or I'll put some there myself. Is this understood?"

Ryu nodded, barely moving his head for fear of upsetting his father. He ate slowly, making sure his body didn't shake or move in any other way then he meant it to. "Yes Father, I'll strive to be better, like Mitsuo."

His father snorted before he glared at Ryu. "No more food. Go into the forest, and don't come back till morning."

Ryu obeyed immediately, got up from the table, and left, never looking back, knowing there was nothing he could do as he heard shouting come from inside the house. He walked out of the village to a small camp, one Mitsuo had set up for him for when this kind of thing happened; he sat against a tree, ignoring everything else as he settled in to sleep.

Just as he was about to drift off, he heard a noise that had him on his feet and reaching for his sword that wasn't there. Realizing he had left it at the house, he fell into a battle stance, but relaxed when a familiar figure walked out of the woods with a kind smile on his face and his arms open.

"Mitsuo!" Ryu threw himself at his brother with a smile, taking in his unique scent that was marred with blood.

"Hello, little brother. I figured Father would send you out here." Ryu nodded against his brother's chest before he backed away, his smile falling.

"Why weren't you at dinner?"

Mitsuo's smile was contagious and soon Ryu was smiling again.

"I was finishing a mission…I only just got back. How have you been faring?" Mitsuo sat down and Ryu shrugged as he followed suit.

"Same as yesterday, big brother!" Mitsuo looked up at the sky; his shinobi shozoku was spotless, despite the smell of blood, and Ryu was jealous. Ryu would always come back filthy, while Mitsuo was perfectly clean. Mitsuo chuckled as he stood up.

"Well, I should be getting home, little brother. I'll come by later with some food since I doubt Father let you eat."

Ryu suddenly had a bad feeling, and somehow knew he had to keep Mitsuo there or something bad would happen. He jumped to his feet and placed himself in front of Mitsuo.

"Do you have to go so soon?"

Mitsuo nodded and moved around him faster than Ryu could follow. "I'll be back with food."

Ryu nodded and sat down as Mitsuo vanished; hours went by but he didn't return. Finally, just as the sun came up, Ryu took off into the forest toward the village. As he burst through the tree line onto the main road, he froze; bodies littered the ground. Friends, family, everyone he knew. The kills were fresh, and for some the light had just started to fade from their eyes, meaning whoever had killed them was fast. As he moved closer and closer to his home, more bodies met his eyes, some dying, most already dead.

"What's happening?"

His question was met with silence as he ran towards his home. He felt like he was knee deep in blood, and when he entered the compound, it wasn't much better. The doors were hacked apart, and bodies were everywhere. He ran through the archway, not bothering to remove his sandals, and hurried into his room, where he ripped his sword from the wall. He pulled it from its sheath with practiced ease, and then he was moving. There was a crash somewhere and he knew he had just lost someone important. "Not Mother, not brother."

He walked through the living area and the sight he came upon horrified him. His mother was there sitting in her knitting chair. A wound through her chest and chair said it had been quick. He shed a tear, but didn't allow himself more than that as his brother's words moved through him, soft and encouraging.

"Never allow your feelings to control you. Always maintain control. If you give in to your feelings, you give in to defeat." So he continued walking, sword poised in front of him, till the sound of swords crossing reached his ears and he took off. A new energy was in his steps and a sudden calm washed over him.

He came upon a scene he had envisioned more than once…his father and brother, murder in both their eyes and swords held in front of them, ready to kill. At first glance he reasoned his father had killed everyone, and then small details registered. His father's blade was clean, not a drop of blood on it, while his brother's was red with it. Mitsuo was fully dressed for battle…their father was dressed for bed.

Ryu dropped his sword as he fell to his knees. "No."

Mitsuo glanced at him out of the comer of his eye before he flashed behind his father and impaled him with a single move. His father smirked as he fell. Mitsuo looked down at the body with disgust.

"Bastard's probably proud that I killed him with a move he taught me; how pathetic."

Mitsuo looked at Ryu and smiled. "Sorry I didn't return with food, little brother." Ryu was shocked as Mitsuo sheathed his jet black sword like nothing had happened.

"Why Mitsuo? Why did you kill everyone?"

Mitsuo looked at him for a long time before he shrugged."You, little brother. You're the reason."

Ryu gaped as he stood up, sword forgotten. "I don't

want this!"

Mitsuo threw back his head and laughed. His laugh had always been deep and pleasant, but now it had an insane edge to it.

"Not for you, because of you. They wanted to take my power; you know how that makes me feel? To have you, a little brat playing ninja, come up and try to take my power? I have earned this power and I wasn't about to hand it over to you, so I killed them. Now they can't transfer the power. It's going to stay mine. The only way I'll lose it is if it finds a better host, and as soon as you lie dead at my feet, there will only be me. Wonderful, isn't it?"

Ryu couldn't comprehend what was happening as Mitsuo grabbed him by the back of his shirt and dragged him through the house and into the middle of the street.

"Here's a good spot. Goodbye, little one." He raised his sword, but right as he was about to bring the full force of the blade down, he suddenly stumbled back, clutching his stomach with a grimace.

"Not now! I only need a few more seconds!" Mitsuo growled as a small blue orb popped out of his chest and slammed into Ryu with enough force to throw him across the street. The last thing he remembered was the smell of blood and the sight of Mitsuo, screaming in the middle of the street, before Ryu knew no more.

***

Ryu bolted upright with a gasp; his vision was blurry and something was restraining him. He looked down and found a hand on his chest, and followed the hand up the arm to a face he knew well.

"Takeo?" His voice was rough and his throat hurt.

Takeo took a glass of water off the nightstand and slowly helped him drink; Ryu lightly shook as Takeo helped him lay back down. "Don't worry Ryu, I'm here."

Ryu coughed as Takeo took a cloth from a bowl and placed it on his forehead, making him feel a thousand times better. "Thank you, Takeo."

Takeo grinned as he nodded. "Anytime, Ryu."

Ryu closed his eyes. "About last night...."

Takeo shook his head as he looked away. "No need, I was out of line."

Ryu shook his head, an effort that hurt more than it should have. "No. I was, Takeo. I'm sorry."

Takeo rolled his eyes. "Fine, apology accepted. Now will you please lie down? You'll recover faster if you lie still." Ryu lay back and looked up at the ceiling, while Takeo dipped the cloth into the bowl, then wrung it out before setting it back on Ryu's head with practiced ease, achieved over many nights like this one. This time the cloth covered his eyes as well.

"Relax and sleep. I'll sit here and make sure nothing happens." Ryu couldn't find the strength to argue as his mind drifted to all the other times the nightmare had come and Takeo had been there with his cup and bowl of cold water, ready to help.

"Takeo, I'll never be able to thank you enough."

Chapter Two:
The Elders

Ryu opened his eyes and looked around. Sunlight streamed in through the window as he sat up, feeling his strained muscles pull with the effort. He groaned softly as he stood up. His sword was on his table, and he was dressed in a white yukata, telling him Mamoru had come in to check on him. He walked to the door and opened it quietly, his anger from the previous night all but gone in light of his dream. He found Takeo and Makoto sitting in the living area, animatedly talking about their battles. Ryu smiled as he hid in the shadows and watched.

Takeo laughed as Makoto described an attack Takeshi had used on him by flailing his arms in the air and making whooshing sounds to describe air. "Then the air was all whoosh and vroom, and then he was all like, 'I am superior in every regard and you are an ant before me.' Then he took off and left me on the roof, where Sensei found me."

Takeo shook his head, chuckling at how easy it was for Makoto to describe how he nearly died like it was nothing. "I wish mine was more colorful. Nori used me like a punching bag and left, saying how I would never be strong enough so long as I let my temper control me; which is bullshit, but whatever."

Makoto nodded smartly as he got up and placed his

hands on his hips. "He's right, you know; you get angry really fast and for no reason."

Takeo snorted as he stood up too. "Bullshit; I always have a good reason to get angry."

Makoto shook his head. "No you don't. What about that time we ran out of ramen and you burned down Sensei's house?"

Takeo glared as he pointed at Makoto. "I clearly marked the last container as mine, and yet he still took it."

Makoto chuckled as he backed toward the door. "About that. It wasn't him Takeo, it was me."

Takeo glared as he pointed at the door. "Run...you have three seconds. One, two...." Makoto was gone, laughing all the way, and Takeo took off after him with a growl and a blast of fire.

Ryu shook his head with a small smile as he turned around to see Mamoru at the dining table with a cup of tea. "They look like they're having fun. You should join them."

Ryu walked over and carefully sat down. "I think I'll pass." He poured himself a cup and sipped, letting the jasmine aroma wash through him, bringing back memories from his early training days.

Mamoru coughed, and Ryu looked up as a folded piece of paper was handed to him. He opened it, and what he saw made his good mood vanish. "The Elders wish to see me?"

Mamoru nodded as Ryu got up and walked toward his door. He opened it and vanished inside, coming back out thirty seconds later dressed in a fresh shinobi shozoku with only his eyes visible. He looked up as he finished fastening his sword on his back to see his sensei with a cane in his hand.

Ryu snorted. "The cane is too much."

Mamoru chuckled as he grabbed the handle and pulled out a hidden two-foot blade with a blue hue to it. "Maybe. But still, it'll save me the trouble of finding one in seventy to eighty years."

Ryu shook his head as his sensei turned around and slashed the air, causing a black cut to appear before rapidly opening to the size of a grown man. "You really think that you're going to live to be in your hundreds?"

Mamoru stopped before the door way and shot a grin over his shoulder. "No, but I'm hoping. Aren't we all?" He stepped through and Ryu shrugged.

"Maybe some, but not all." He walked through the rip in the dimension and was immediately engulfed in darkness. He moved forward until he saw another rip in front of him, leading to another separate dimension, one of many that lay parallel to the one they were normally in. He stepped out into a barren landscape.

The ground under his feet was cracked and the sky above was streaked with clouds red like blood. In front of him was a flight of stairs that stretched towards the heavens, with four hundred steps and four gates, one placed at every hundred steps. "Flashy and evil looking as always." Ryu looked at his sensei, who was grinning.

"Yeah, it reflects the people inside. Wouldn't you agree?"

Ryu nodded as they started walking up the stairs. They came to the first gate, where a man greeted them, wearing red battle armor like a samurai and a naginata clutched in his right hand. He waved and they stopped. "Summoned?"

He held out his hand and Ryu handed him the paper. The man looked at it. "This way."

He led them to the left of the gate to a small door, where he pulled out a knife and cut his palm before placing it on the door. As soon as his hand made contact, the door opened to an elaborate room. "They're waiting." The man walked off and Ryu was the first to walk through.

Ryu looked around the room; it looked like a mausoleum with tall pillars that vanished toward the black ceiling. Mamoru walked next to him and the door they walked through vanished, revealing a long walkway that led to a set of double doors at the other end. "Well, well, well, how nice of you to finally show."

Ryu gritted his teeth at the dark tone. He turned around to see three thrones, side by side, all occupied with men dressed for battle. The one in the middle was tall with medium black hair. His beard and mustache had been trimmed, and he was wearing sleek black armor. His face was set in a cruel smirk, and his black eyes were alight with glee, as if he knew how much Ryu despised him and knew the young ninja could do nothing about it. His hands were clasped together on the hilt of a sword that was embedded in the floor in front of him; the blade itself was black with a wavy design, and seemed to hum the closer Ryu got to it.

The man on his right was dressed in red armor like the guard, but his armor was made of better material. He had short black hair that was kept out of his eyes with a red headband. His face was clean shaven and seemed to be made of stone. He clutched a spear in his right hand that was standing straight up. His brown eyes gazed at Ryu with no emotion whatsoever.

The man on the far left was sitting sideways in his chair, a carefree expression on his face as if nothing bothered him. His brown hair was semi-short and wild, and stuck out in every direction like he had just been shocked. His green eyes followed Ryu with a predatory glee, as if he were a hunter that had just found its next meal.

Ryu looked at them each in turn, starting with the man in the middle.

"Lord Nobunaga Oda...." The black haired man nodded and Ryu looked to his left at the samurai.

"Lord Ieyasu Tokugawa...." The man, also with black hair, returned his nod and Ryu looked at the wild man.

"Lord Hideyoshi Toyotomi...." The brown haired man cocked his head up in acknowledgment.

Mamoru bowed, and had to force Ryu to follow suit. When the formalities were done, Hideyoshi laughed.

"Get that stick out of your ass Mamoru, the brat doesn't have to bow."

Mamoru gave a half bow. "Of course, Lord Toyotomi."

Ryu rolled his eyes as he stepped forward. "You summoned me." He ground the words out as if they were poison, and Nobunaga's smirk turned wicked.

"Yes, we understand that you have not yet accepted your destiny and shared a bed with Ieyasu's descendent."

Ryu shook his head, his hand itching for his sword. "No, I've made this clear. I have not, nor will I ever accept the bond."

Nobunaga chuckled as he stood up, taking his sword with him as he approached Ryu. "Of course you haven't, I was just making sure you were still being a sad excuse for a progeny."

Nobunaga raised his sword to block Ryu's as he growled. "I am nobody's puppet, is that clear?" Ryu attacked again and again, but Nobunaga's sword was always ready to intercept.

"I understand that's what you're saying, but that doesn't mean you're free to choose your own destiny. We made a deal with the kami, and we are honor bound to make sure you do what we promised."

Ryu's eyes flashed black as he lashed out, throwing Nobunaga back. The shocked man recovered with a snort. "Tsk tsk, still such a disapp—"

Ryu cut him with a slash from his sword, which barely touched his armor, but still managed to throw him back again. "Fuck you and fuck the Kami. I AM NO ONES BITCH! Is that fucking clear? I will do what I want, when I want, and if you have a problem with that, then you can go straight to hell." Ryu turned around and stormed off, leaving four shocked men behind.

Mamoru shook his head as he turned towards the council. "Forgive him please, a thousand pardons. He has been through a lot, he just needs more time." Nobunaga took his seat, a glare directed at Mamoru. He ran his hand over his armor and the damage was gone.

"How much longer, Hattori? We don't have forever, you know. Susanoo himself came to me. They reminded me of the prophecy, and also how they can make all the power vanish. We did not make a deal with the Kami only for your student to make us mortal men again. Remember that, Mamoru, because if we fall, we'll take your students with us."

Mamoru clenched his hands as he nodded and turned to leave, but just as he started walking he heard Oda speak. "Mamoru, Zenaku's asking about you."

Mamoru whirled around and fixed shocked eyes on Nobunaga. "Why?"

Nobunaga shrugged. "It's our power that hides you from him. If he finds you...well, let's just hope nothing happens to our power. Eh?"

Mamoru nodded mutely as he turned toward the big doors and took off running.

***

Ryu slammed the doors behind him. *I am nobody's puppet!*

He growled and debated going back in, but decided against it. Better to be thought a child than to walk back in like a kicked puppy.

The doors opened and the sensei walked out, pale. Ryu snorted. "Ripped you a new one so bad you suffered blood loss, huh?"

Mamoru chuckled, slightly shaken. "Yes, I guess they did."

Ryu's eyes narrowed as they started walking down the stairs and through the large doors that opened as they approached.

"Ryu, do you know why the Elders are so strong?"

Ryu shrugged as he stared at the sky. "Yeah, they made a deal with Amaterasu, the goddess of the sun, Tsukiyomi the god of the moon, and Susanoo the god of storms. Why? Is that important?"

Mamoru nodded as they walked through the second gate. "Yes, it's important; they are the ones that gave a portion of their power to the Elders, not only over elements but also immortality. But these came at a cost; do you know what that was?"

Ryu shrugged again as they walked through the third gate. "Yeah, they promised that they would pass on the power to their kids and that their kids would pass it on, so in short they became the original Three, the warriors that the Kami would call on in times of great need. When they couldn't directly interfere, they would call on the Three and they would stop whatever calamity threatened the world."

Mamoru nodded as they walked through the last gate and started heading toward the ground. "Yes, very well, but do you know why their children must be together?"

Ryu growled as he glared at the ground. "It was a pact they made when they received the power. They swore that their lines would always be together. But when they did this, the Kami—Inari Okami—played a trick on them by altering the oath and turning it romantic, where they had meant it to be a brotherhood. Unfortunately, since they had sworn on holy power, they had to honor it or they would lose their immortality. So now when the power passes from one vessel to the next, they try to pimp the kids together so they can be young forever."

Mamoru shook his head. "No, they bring the children together so that the Kami will have the warriors they need, should they need them."

Ryu snorted as they approached the spot they had entered in. "Whatever you say, Sensei. If I ever meet the Kami, they are going to get a hell of an earful."

Mamoru sighed as he pulled out his sword and created another rip. This time Ryu walked through first and was instantly back in the kitchen, followed by Mamoru.

"Now why can't you do that every time?"

Mamoru shrugged. "It takes too much energy, but I figured this time it wouldn't matter, 'cause I'm off to bed."

He walked off to a door on the far side of the room. Ryu walked to his own door and decided a nap was definitely in order. He dressed down into his yukata again and could hear Makoto and Takeo shouting outside. "Hours pass in the Elder Dimension while minutes pass here. I guess time does fly when you're getting chewed out." He slowly drifted off, thinking exactly what he would say if he was ever in the presence of the Kami.

***

Ryu walked through the double doors; he felt stronger, the doors caved on themselves as his aura brushed against them. "I'm like a god." He looked down at his hands to see black spidery veins branching off in all directions; he walked toward the thrones, where three men were ready for battle.

Nobunaga growled. "I knew you were nothing but a monster." He brandished his sword in front of him.

Ryu smirked, his black eyes alight with power. "Monster? Huh, is that what I am? I thought I was a god."

He vanished and reappeared behind Nobunaga, grabbing the black sword and impaling Nobunaga on it with a grin. "But I do enjoy killing, so maybe there is some credence to your theory; but I like mine better."

He grabbed the blade and cut his ancestor in half before he turned to the other shocked Elders, Nobunaga's sword in hand. "Anyone else?" Hideyoshi was next, thrusting his trident at Ryu, while Ieyasu came in from behind. Ryu threw the sword in the air before grabbing both of the weapons coming at him and letting them skim along his body. He turned sideways, forcing them through their allies' bodies, and they looked down at their teammate's weapons that had them impaled.

Ryu caught Nobunaga's sword and with barely a flick, decapitated both of them. He cackled, throwing his head back, and the room shook with the insane laughter. He walked back to the double doors and saw an army, one that had followed him all the way there.

Mitsuo and Mamoru led the charge as they tried to stop him. Ryu grinned as he ran at them, meeting them at the second gate. Mitsuo was the first to engage him. "Brother, don't give in! Fight it! Fight the beast! Don't let it control you!"

Ryu shook his head, the evil smirk still in place. "Don't you understand, brother? I'm the most powerful entity in this world. I have enough power to challenge the Kami. Join me; we could rule everything. You could rule earth and I'll rule heaven."

Mitsuo shook his head as he held his blade in front of him, the katana pointed at Ryu's heart. Ryu nodded and attacked with his ancestor's sword, and Mitsuo met the attack head on. They battled back and forth at intense speeds before they both stopped. Nobunaga's blade was through Mitsuo's heart and Ryu was smirking. "I told you, I have become a kami. You could've fought beside me, but instead you chose them."

His smirk faded and his eyes turned back to their regular lightning blue. "Why couldn't you choose me just once? Why couldn't you choose your family?" Ryu pulled his sword out and Mitsuo fell dead at his feet.

Mamoru growled as he attacked Ryu head on, but Ryu took the thrust through his heart before turning his gaze on Mamoru. With a single flick of his sword Ryu sent Mamoru's head flying away from his body, the blade slid out of Ryu's chest, and the faceless army stopped. Ryu growled. "Fuck them all, I'll rule this world by myself." He thrust his sword toward the sky and a crash of thunder was the only warning before the world was bathed in lightning.

***

Ryu bolted upward; a cold sweat had broken over his skin and he was panting. "What the hell was that?" But he

51

couldn't stay awake and lay back down, asleep before he even hit the pillow.

***

Mamoru sat at the table drinking tea as the sun started to set. He felt a presence hiding in the shadows and gestured at an empty seat across from him. "Don't worry, Ryu is asleep and the other two are running an errand. I figured you'd want to talk."

The figure walked forward with a nod, his faded blue eyes focused on the tea that Mamoru offered. "What brings you to my humble home, Mitsuo?"

Mitsuo held up his hand at the tea and Mamoru pulled it back. "How is he?"

Mamoru shrugged as he set the tea down and picked up his own cup. "He's fine; he had the nightmare last night, but Takeo took care of it."

Mitsuo sat down without making a sound. "Yes, I figured as much. Seeing me usually brings those memories to the surface."

Mamoru nodded as he placed his own cup on the table. "Yes; plus we got a call from the council, and I believe he's having the nightmare again. He was screaming an hour ago, but it's stopped now."

Mitsuo gritted his teeth. "Good, he'll need that hatred if he's going to do what I need him to."

Mamoru sighed as he shook his head. "You really need to stop pushing him. There's only so much he can take before he cracks again."

Mitsuo sighed as he looked at the door that was separating his brother from him. "I know I pushed too much last night. And I was forced to fight that demon for a full minute."

Mamoru nodded as he pulled out a small notebook and wrote something down. "A full minute; that hasn't happened since he was first told that he had a destiny that he couldn't control." He put the notebook back in his yukata as Mitsuo sighed.

"I need him to understand what's inside him. I wish I could just tell him, but that would ruin everything."

Mamoru nodded as he looked toward the front door, expecting his students back any second. "Don't worry, Mitsuo. As long as I can keep the council away from him, he'll be fine."

Mitsuo glared as his gaze snapped to Mamoru. "What did they want?"

Mamoru shook his head as he turned back to Mitsuo, but Mitsuo slammed his fist onto the table and Mamoru knew keeping this a secret was not an option. "They threatened to reveal my location to Zenaku."

Mitsuo barely showed any shock but slightly grimaced. "If he finds them, he'll kill them. Mamoru, they have to survive. The plan can't work without them. No matter the price, they have to survive." Mamoru was about to argue but the front door opened, so he turned around to greet his students as Mitsuo vanished out the back door.

Mamoru glanced over his shoulder at the darkness in the corner of his patio and nodded. As soon as he did the darkness was gone and he felt a sick feeling in the pit of his stomach. *Things are only going to get worse.*

Chapter Three:
Beasts and Burdens

Makoto laughed as Takeo ran around the room, running from Ryu, who seemed dead set on killing him for throwing a ramen noodle at him. Makoto couldn't stop smiling; whatever was wrong with his family, he felt it was slowly righting itself. Several weeks had gone by and Ryu was starting to laugh again, Takeo wasn't punching through walls anymore, and even Mamoru seemed to be in better moods. All in all, his family, whatever was wrong with it, was now getting better. "Makoto, help me! Your deranged boyfriend can't take a joke!"

Makoto shouted at the same time that Ryu did. "I'm not his boyfriend!" Makoto blushed and Ryu growled and stormed out.

Takeo flopped down on the couch with a grin. "Whew! Works every time. OW!"

Makoto stuck his nose in the air and walked out of the house as Takeo nursed his bruised shin.

Makoto walked into the garden to find Ryu leaning against the tree, looking up at the full moon. Makoto stayed back, knowing Ryu's distance boundaries. "Beautiful, isn't it?"

Makoto looked at Ryu, surprised he was the one to start the conversation. "Yeah, it's stunning."

Ryu looked over his shoulder at Makoto and tilted his head to say. "Come here."

Makoto walked forward slowly, like he was approaching a dangerous animal, and in a sense, he was. Ryu was the strongest and the deadliest among them…that's why he was the leader.

"I sometimes wonder if Tsukiyomi is watching us in the night. I feel a presence, a…safety net, like a blanket."

Makoto looked at Ryu as he continued staring at the moon.

"On nights like this I know there's nothing to worry about, because Tsukiyomi is watching us. It's nights with clouds, or nights of the new moon, that I worry, 'cause his gaze is gone for one reason or another."

Makoto stayed silent, not wanted to break whatever trance Ryu had fallen into.

"Like that night when I fought Mitsuo, when the clouds would part and his light would shine on me, I felt stronger and I was able to dodge Mitsuo's attacks easier. Then the clouds would block his view and I felt vulnerable again, like Susanoo was trying to stop him from protecting me. Heh." He turned to Makoto with a sad smile. "Maybe I'm just making excuses for my own weakness. Blaming the Kami for what's wrong with my life."

Makoto shook his head. "No Ryu, I believe they watch and help when they can, but heal when they can't."

Ryu nodded as he turned away from the moon, casting his face in shadows. "It's nice to hear that I might not be crazy, maybe I'm not weak, and the Kami really are helping."

Makoto nodded eagerly. "Of course they are. You couldn't be weak Ryu. Your speed is unmatched by me or Takeo, and even Mamoru-sensei has a hard time keeping up with you. Plus, your strength is unparalleled by anyone I know."

Ryu snorted as he started walking back toward the

house. "Maybe you're right, maybe you're wrong. I'm not the right person to ask. I have way too many issues." And just like that the wall slammed shut and left Makoto in the cold, while Ryu retreated into himself.

Takeo chuckled at the TV as it showed the weather. Even after the carnage from their last mission, the clans had cleaned it up, and now, besides one missing CEO for Nakamura Tech, they didn't find dismembered bodies on any rooftops. Nothing was happening in the world, aside from the freak lightning storm from several weeks ago that had downed three city blocks. *Ryu would fry the TV if he heard them call him a freak.*

Takeo got up as he shut off the TV and went into the dining room, where Mamoru was looking at a scroll. "Another mission, Sensei?"

Mamoru nodded as he rolled up the scroll. "Yes, the council seems to like keeping you three busy."

Takeo shrugged. "Nothing new. But I'm not sure it's wise to send Ryu or Makoto out, not so soon."

Mamoru nodded slowly before he handed the scroll to Takeo. "Can you handle this by yourself? It's from the Chozou clan. Apparently a member of the Tenzou clan is seeing the daughter of Hajime Chozou. Her name in Mayumi, and Hajime has asked the council for the Right of Execution, which they granted and passed to us, so now it's our job to see that...." Mamoru looked at the scroll before continuing. "Michio Tenzou is dead by morning."

Takeo bobbed his head as he grabbed the scroll that was offered, and left to get ready. He walked into his room and grinned; it had been awhile since he had been on a mission by himself, and it was a little exciting. He grabbed his sword off its hook and changed into his shinobi shozoku before looking at himself in the mirror. *Takeo Toyotomi, Lord of Fire. Master of executions.*

He chuckled as he left through his window. His wings sprouted from his back, sending a shock down his spine.

57

This is the life. He took off into the sky, heading towards Mount Fuji.

***

Makoto walked into the house to find only Mamoru present. "Where did everyone go?"

Mamoru looked up with a smile. "They're out on missions; there's one for you, too."

Makoto walked forward and sat down across from his sensei. "What kind of mission?"

Mamoru grabbed a scroll and read it. "It seems like the council is worried over a clan of vampires that are moving too close to the city. Ah, they want the clan to move ten miles farther away from the city, and if they refuse they are to be wiped out."

Makoto nodded, not used to dealing with the supernatural races, but that was just a marker he had to pass. "Of course Sensei, I'll take care of it."

Makoto grabbed the scroll and walked toward his room, before he turned around. "What mission did Ryu get?"

Mamoru cocked his eyebrow and Makoto blushed slightly. "I mean, I don't want him to over exert himself so soon after what happened."

Mamoru nodded slowly. "He has to handle a clan of werewolves who are trying to expand their territory, same parameters as yours. Obey, or die."

Makoto nodded before he left, leaving Mamoru to sigh. "Sorry Takeo, the world doesn't wait for the weary."

***

Ryu stormed in with a face of stone, seconds after Takeo vanished into his room. Ryu walked up to Mamoru and slammed his hands on the table. "Mission."

Mamoru cleared his throat and Ryu growled. "Mission. Please."

He ground out the words and Mamoru nodded, handing Ryu a scroll. "Pretty simple, all you have to do...." Ryu stalked off to his room and closed the door, leaving Mamoru to nod his head.

"Is read it yourself.... Okay then." He went back to his tea as Makoto walked in.

Mamoru shook his head. "They never take enough down time." He sighed again and set about the difficult task of drowning himself in his tea.

***

Ryu landed with a thud, not bothering to keep himself hidden. He knew the werewolves knew he was there, and when three huge wolves came running towards him from a mountain range, he double checked that he had a silver dagger with him.

The lead wolf stopped in front of him before morphing back into a man. He was Ryu's height with a mane of shaggy brown hair; his kin were beside him, one black as night, and the other reddish brown. The one in human form greeted Ryu with a grin. "You must be one of the Three; we have heard a lot about you."

He held out a hand that Ryu only looked at. "Alright, fair warning though. Walking into a werewolf den with anything silver won't make you any friends." The man let his hand drop.

Ryu shook his head slightly. "I have been ordered to resolve the situation, and if I can't, I have been ordered to kill you all."

The two wolves crouched and growled, but the human held up his hand. "Fair enough. I'm confident we can resolve this peacefully."

Ryu snorted. "I'll be the judge of that. Tell me what's wrong."

The human nodded. "Well, it started a month ago. A clan from the north, the Grey Pack, started moving in on our territory, marking our trees, taking our game, and drinking from our water. We want them to stop; we have a hard enough time getting by without them making it worse."

Ryu absorbed the information and started walking in the

direction the wolves had come from; the others fell in step next to him. "Why don't they just move? I'm sure there are better sources for their needs. Or they could integrate into the city...get jobs and become citizens."

The man shook his head. "No, werewolves can't; we need to live with our clans in a den of some kind...trees, caves, or in the Grey Packs case, an abandoned castle. We can't live in a human den; too much clutter, too many threats."

Ryu sighed as they approached a cave made in the side of the mountain, and when they walked through the opening Ryu was surprised at what he found. On the inside there were shelves carved out of the rock, big enough to fit Mamoru's house and a good portion of his garden as well.

"Hmm, pretty impressive." The man smirked as his companions jumped up to one of the shelves and watched Ryu from ten feet up.

"Thanks. It took awhile to carve those into the mountain, but we live comfortably. Oh my, I'm sorry. I never introduced myself...my name is Victor. My companions are..."

Ryu held up a hand to stall his words. "I'm Ryu, and I don't need to know your friends' names. I only need to know where to find this Grey Pack, so I can decide which clan needs to die to preserve peace."

Victor nodded with a grim look. "They're in the east, and I'm afraid you may be right; keep in mind though, should you decide our clan has to die...we will fight you to the last."

Ryu nodded and turned around to leave. "I wouldn't expect anything less. I'll be back with my verdict. If I don't return that means your pack is in the clear." He walked back into the night and took off into the sky, heading east.

***

Takeo landed on the mountain near a small, secluded village. "So, this is Chozou village. Huh, Toyotomi was more impressive." He felt a spike of sadness over his lost home, but he shook his head and took off into the village; small shops and houses for a society perfectly happy to dwell in the old days, rather than modernize their lives.

Of course, I'm not much better. I'm living in a house that looks like it came from the Ming dynasty. He chuckled as he walked toward the largest building, hoping Hajime was the kind of self-serving guy Takeo thought he was. As soon as he knocked he knew he was right, because a male servant answered the door. "What is your business?"

Takeo held up the scroll and the servant let him in, before leading him through a long hall with eight doors on each side, all traditional. The walls were brown, and judging by the looks of them, paper thin, like the doors. "Your master has a nice home."

The servant didn't answer; he only led Takeo down the hall to a gold filigree door that was diamond encrusted, with a single emerald for a handle; this was the only solid door in the hall. Takeo whistled. "Damn! I'm in the wrong business."

The servant opened the door, and what Takeo saw quickly made him change his mind. Sitting in a chair was a man dressed in a robe, with thick sausage like fingers, small, beady little eyes, and a handful of hair on his head. *Yikes! Traded looks for money. Never mind, I* am *in the right business.*

The man raised a thick hand and beckoned him forward. *Don't eat me. Please don't eat me.* Takeo stopped three feet from the man, feeling out of place in the extravagant room; whereas the rest of the house was plain, this room was decorated with thick, jeweled furs and long gold-spun tapestries; three pillars held the roof up, each jeweled all the way to the ceiling. "How do you like my home?" The man spoke, his big belly shaking with each word, and Takeo bowed.

"It's very...gold, sir." Takeo offered with a nod.

The man chortled, his chair creaking every time he

moved. "The Chozou clan has been blessed with many successful ventures, including bought land that had a secret gold mine. Between you and me, it was only a secret to the old owners." He chortled some more as Takeo nodded.

Thought so, his physical repulsiveness is only matched by the ugliness of his soul.

The man heaved himself to his feet with great effort, and his chair seemed to sigh. "I am Hajime Chozou, and I require your aid."

Takeo nodded as he produced the scroll. "Yes I know; if you will tell me where Michio is, I'll bring his head as proof."

Hajime shook his head. "No! I don't want him dead."

Takeo was taken aback. "But sir, your scroll says you want him beheaded and brought before you."

Hajime shook his beefy head again. "No, I want him mutilated, then decapitated. I want you to cut him into so many little pieces, it'll look like he went through a meat grinder. Twice."

Takeo sighed as he nodded. "As you wish. One execution is, as you know, one thousand gold pieces." He smiled politely. "If you'll tell me where he is, I'll bring him to you in a body bag."

Hajime nodded before he held up one finger. "Yes, yes. You will receive payment, when I receive the body." He pointed to a sack by his chair, "Also, make that two bags; one for him and one for my daughter."

Takeo's eyes widened as he looked at the scroll. "Her execution isn't authorized, sir."

Hajime waved his hand dismissively. "Pshaw. I know you're one of the Three. You can do it without any issues, just say she got in the way. If you do, I might just part with some of what you see." He gestured at the expensive items around him, as if inviting Takeo to take what he would.

Takeo shook his head with a grimace. "No sir, I have permission to execute one Michio Tenzou, not Mayumi

Chozou."

Hajime scowled. "Listen, I hired you and until you do your job, I own you. So do as I say and kill the little bitch. I will not lose my fortune to that little whore."

Takeo inhaled, controlling his temper before speaking. "Sir, I cannot kill your daughter. I do not have the council's permission, and she has not threatened me. Therefore, I cannot so much as touch her. Now Michio I have the right to kill, but not your daughter. I cannot stress this enough."

Hajime growled before he smirked. "Then say she attacked you...it's that simple. Michio and that bitch will die, and I part with a few items. The money is easy and you get it all."

Takeo was the one who growled as the restraint on his anger snapped. "Money has no fucking use to me! I don't need all this crap, and even if I did, I wouldn't kill an innocent to get it. Now, I'm afraid that, by council rule, I have to kill you for the several crimes you just admitted to."

Hajime backed away. "What? You can't kill me! I haven't done anything wrong!"

Takeo pulled his sword from its sheathe. "Actually, by your own admittance you stole from people, you falsified an assassination contract, and you tried to bribe me; these are three strikes against you."

Hajime opened his mouth, but Takeo made one slash and sheathed his sword as he walked out of the room, leaving Hajime to fall in half and splatter on his gold carpet. "Scum." Takeo walked away, not bothering to look back.

***

Makoto flew through the air, gliding on a current he created as he followed the directions on the scroll. So far he had been flying due east and he had nothing but water below him and water stretching as far as he could see, but then the world suddenly shifted and his instincts kicked in. He lashed out, throwing blades of air in every direction, but they didn't hit anything and just continued going. Makoto looked around and let out a relieved sigh. What he had perceived as an attack was, in fact, just a protective barrier that was meant to turn away mortals so they wouldn't see a giant floating castle fifty feet above the water.

He landed on the floating island, walked to the great double doors, and knocked, his breath coming slow and steady. The doors opened with an eerie groan and a pale woman answered, wearing a blood red dress, her blood red lipstick standing out against her complexion. "Oh hello, you look positively yummy." She licked her lips and Makoto tensed as he held out the scroll. She took it with a curious tilt to her head.

She read the scroll before pouting cutely. "Oh, you're here on business. That's too bad. Well, come in." She stepped to the side and Makoto walked in, mindful of everything.

The inside was stunningly beautiful. The room was covered in darkness. A staircase led to a door, then branched off to the left and the right. There were ten rooms on each side of the ground floor, and it was obviously old, older than anything Makoto had ever seen.

"You have a very lovely home."

She looked at him before nodding her head. "I can see you really mean that...it's a little surprising. Most can't understand a vampire's unique taste in decoration."

Makoto nodded as the woman appeared beside him. "Ryu would love it...he's into the dark Goth thing."

She smiled as she led him up the stairs. "He sounds delightful; is he your boyfriend?"

Makoto blushed as he shook his head. "No, no, nothing like that. He's just a friend."

She nodded as they reached the landing. "You sound fond of him."

Makoto nodded with a wistful smile. "Yeah, I am, but, he's...just untouchable. It's a dark, forbidden thing he has going for him."

She smiled sadly as she shook her head. "I never could understand why mortals deny themselves something they want. Your lives are too short to deny yourselves. Oh well, mortal issues are not immortal problems. I'm Cassandra; let me know if you need something."

She gestured to the door and it opened to a room much like the one he was standing in, Makoto turned to her but she was gone. "Uh, thank you?" He shrugged and walked into the room. As soon as the doors shut, torches burst to life and a man appeared sitting in a throne. His red eyes narrowed slightly, as if he were critically examining a piece of art. His long silver hair shone in the light from the torches, setting the color on fire.

Makoto swallowed as he walked toward the man; judging from the way he was sitting he was of aristocrat descent. His boots were black and beautifully made; small details made them stand out, tiny scuffs said they were well used, and silver buckles held them closed. He wore a pair of black pants—silk from the way the light shone off them— matched by a silk shirt, and he was wearing a faded black cloak with two tails on the shoulders, suggesting it was really old. Makoto ended his examination on his eyes, which sparkled with amusement.

"See something you like, mortal?"

Makoto shivered as his voice washed over him, like liquid lust. His voice was low, dark, and promised pain, but at the same time, spoke of a pleasure only he could give you. Makoto shook his head, clearing it. "I'm Makoto Tokugawa; I have been sent by the Elders."

The man straightened up. "Yes, I figured as much. But I never expected that the Elders would send one of the Three. I'm humbled that they considered me to be problem enough for one of the Three, but I'm afraid I made myself perfectly clear when I last spoke with them. We cannot move any further, so if those old fools want us any further, they are going to have to move the humans."

65

Makoto grimaced as he reached for his sword and unsheathed it. "I'm sorry, but if you refuse, I have to kill you."

The man nodded as he stood up. "I'm being rude, I haven't introduced myself. I am Count Leonhardt van Hellsing...no relation to the hunter. Most call me Leon; I would appreciate if you did too."

Makoto nodded as Leon sat back down and sighed. "Now that the pleasantries are out of the way, back to this nasty bit of business. I will tell you what I told the council; we cannot move from this location."

Makoto walked forward with his sword in hand. "Why? How hard can it be to move a flying castle?"

Leon chuckled. "It's a lot harder than you would think, and I'm afraid my clan is too small to do it now."

Makoto cautiously sheathed his sword. "What happened?"

Leon smiled sadly. "Ah! The last war happened; you would've been too young to fight in it. It happened fifteen years ago." He got a faraway look in his eyes. "It was quite the collection. Werewolves, vampire, ninja, dragons...oh, we were all there, fighting a nameless foe; we called them the Black Hand. Unbelievably powerful foes: each one had the strength, speed, and endurance of ten men. They were terrifying. But then the Three appeared...ah, they were stunning. Never have I seen a more gifted incarnation. One came from the heavens encased in fire, a trident in one hand, and with the other he called down storms of fire. Then another came. One second he wasn't there, and then he was. Lightning danced around him as if it were a party. And finally the last came riding a tornado. With them the battle changed, and where once it was a one sided massacre, now it was a battle. To this day, I don't know how they changed the direction we were heading, but they inspired confidence, power, strength. You name it, they brought it in spades."

He blinked and then his eyes focused on Makoto. "Ah,

I'm sorry; I got lost in my memories."

Makoto nodded as he stood away from the vampire lord. "Well, maybe I could help."

A shocked look came over Leon. "No! I couldn't ask that; you are supposed to make us fix our problem, not help us."

Makoto shook his head, the idea sounding better and better. "No, if you'll have me. I would be glad to help."

Leon seemed to consider it before he stood up and bowed deeply. "We would be forever in your debt."

Makoto blushed as Leon stood and led him back into the main room. "I can move the barrier, but I'm afraid that is the extent of my powers."

Makoto nodded as they walked down the steps, very aware of the man beside him. *What have I gotten myself into?*

***

Ryu dropped from the sky into a forest, using the branches to reach the ground. When he landed he found himself in a meadow with eyes all around him. "I'm looking for the leader of the Grey Pack."

Three wolves dropped out of the trees surrounding him; one morphed while he fell and landed on all fours before he straightened up. His body was dirty and small branches and leaves were in his hair. "What businesses have you with Witherfang?" His words came out as a growl, and from past experiences, Ryu was sure he spent most of his time as a wolf.

"The Elders sent me."

The wolves exchanged glances before nodding. The human nodded to Ryu. "You, follow."

He morphed into a wolf and he and some of the pack ran towards a castle that could barely be seen. Ryu ran with them, keeping up despite them obviously trying to lose him, and before long they came to the castle.

When they went in Ryu knew there was something

67

different. All the wolves he had met so far had come up to his chest; the one inside waiting for him on a dais towered over him. Ryu felt a genuine shock of fear as he realized exactly what he was standing in front of. He bowed deeply.

"Rise mortal." Ryu stood up and found the wolf still before him. "Yes. I am an ancient one."

Ryu bowed again. "Forgive me, but I have never before been blessed with meeting an ancient one. My lord, forgive my impertinence."

The great wolf stood ten feet fall, and was as grey as the stone around him. His bright yellow eyes spoke to the fact that he was one of the few that made the change and never went back. "That is alright. Most don't know what to do when they come upon one of us. The way in which you recovered so quickly is surprising in one so young."

Ryu quickly bowed before standing straight. "Thank you, my lord; I'm afraid I have been sent by the Elders."

The great wolf inclined its head and Ryu pulled out the scroll and unfurled it. "My lord, I have been tasked by the Elders to preserve peace, before the mundane begin to investigate any and all occurrences in the area."

The wolf nodded as he walked forward, his steps shaking the walls around them. "Preserve peace in what capacity?"

Ryu swallowed as the wolf walked closer. "Deadly force has been authorized."

The wolf gave no signs of aggression, he just bobbed his great head, which was the size of Ryu's torso. "Do you know why?" The wolf's deep voice boomed even while he was calm.

Ryu shook his head as the beast started circling him. "No my lord, I don't; nor do I question why. I was sent here to find a peaceful solution, and if I can't, I will terminate one of the packs."

The wolf nodded as it sat in front of him. "You follow orders. But, do you ever wonder why they are there?"

Ryu shook his head resolutely. "No my lord, I don't question, I carry out my orders to the letter. I have never disobeyed a direct order unless it affects me directly. Now will you or will you not coexist with the pack to the west?"

The wolf looked at Ryu for a long time before he nodded. "No, and yes. We will simply move; if we wish to expand our territory, we shall move our pack farther east. Is this satisfactory?"

Ryu thought about it before he nodded. "Yes, that will do fine, my lord."

The great wolf nodded before cocking his head. "The children call me Witherfang; in my eyes you are a child."

Ryu turned to leave. "Thank you, Lord Witherfang, for compromising for the sake of peace."

He didn't see Witherfang's response, but Witherfang did speak. "Remember, some orders, no matter how nicely worded, have only one purpose...." Ryu stopped and turned his head to show he was listening. "The only purpose they serve is to make you less human; to make you a monster."

Witherfang was regarding him with an unreadable expression before Ryu bowed. "Thank you for your words of wisdom, Lord Witherfang. I will keep them at the forefront of my mind at all times."

Witherfang bowed slightly and Ryu returned it before he took off into the sky, eager to leave the place and those words behind. *A monster, huh?*

***

Takeo landed in the front yard and walked through his sensei's front door just as something flew out the back door. Takeo pulled out his sword and ran after it, but just as he got to the threshold, Mamoru appeared with a grin. "Where's the fire?"

Takeo looked around his sensei but there was nothing there, so he sheathed his blade. "Nothing Sensei. I thought I saw something."

Mamoru shook his head as he looked around

incredulously. "Nope, just you and me in this old house."

Takeo looked at his sensei. "What about the other two?"

Mamoru shrugged. "I'm sorry Takeo, but I can't give them special attention."

Takeo gritted his teeth, but nodded understanding as he sat down. "Still, I think we need a few days off after this."

His sensei nodded. "Maybe a break is what you need." Mamoru sat down across from him. "After they get back we'll take a break. There's something I need to teach you all anyways."

Takeo perked up at the prospect of training. "Sounds good, Sensei!"

***

Makoto stood at the edge of the island looking down at the sea as it turned and rolled violently. Leonhardt van Hellsing stood next to him, his cloak billowing in the breeze. "Are you sure you want to help?"

Makoto nodded as he leapt into the sky. He flipped in mid air and looked at the floating island; it seemed so simple and yet it felt impossible. Makoto shook his head violently before he stretched out both of his arms and gale force winds started roaring, whipping around him. He pulled it closer and closer, letting the wind tear around him, screaming in his ears. When he couldn't hold the power anymore, he threw it all at the island.

At first nothing happened, and then slowly the island started moving farther and farther. The more Makoto put into it, the faster it moved and the weaker he got. Finally he broke his connection and the wind faded, the island only a small speck.

Makoto heaved for breath as his eyes closed. He felt like he had physically moved the island; his wings pounded furiously but his body refused to stay aloft, and he fell straight toward the sea. He was falling, but he felt good…tired, but good.

He opened his eyes and found himself looking into

darkness, and the scent of blood was all around. "Not bad mortal. Not bad at all." Makoto tilted his head and found himself nestled against Leonhardt's body as they glided back to the island.

"My clansmen and I will owe you a debt, one that you may take in any way you find satisfactory."

Makoto let his eyes shut. "I'll hold you to that, Leonhardt van Hellsing." He felt himself drifting off into unconsciousness as Leon laughed into the wind.

***

Ryu landed on the roof of his sensei's house. The moon shone overhead, and he felt shaken to his core and yet calm at the same time. *Question some orders?*

He snorted; without orders there was only chaos. Life without rules and restrictions equaled chaos and destruction; he back flipped off the roof and landed in front of the front door. *Maybe Mamoru will help me understand.* Ryu started to walk in and found his sensei still up.

Mamoru looked up with a smile. "Ahh, so that's two back to the roost. I wonder how my last bird is doing."

Ryu stopped, one foot barely in the door. "Who hasn't returned?"

Mamoru coughed out a word and looked away from Ryu. "I'm sorry Sensei, I didn't quite get that." Ryu's eyes narrowed at Mamoru.

Mamoru sighed as he turned towards Ryu. "Makoto. I sent him to Leonhardt to help him with something."

Ryu froze, his blood running cold. "Leonhardt van Hellsing?"

Mamoru nodded and Ryu took off, running out the door and into the sky, faster than Mamoru could blink. "You know, no matter how much he denies it, he cares for Makoto." Mamoru went back to his tea with a smile.

***

Ryu flew to the exact location of the Black Tower, but it was gone. He swirled around and finally found a small speck

71

in the distance. He shot towards it and found what he was looking for. He flew at the doors, hitting them with enough force to send them across the hall to bounce against the steps. He landed in the main room just as thirty vampires surrounded him. "I'm looking for Makoto; how many die between me and him?"

The vampires parted as Leonhardt stepped forward. "No blood needs to spill. He's upstairs, past the broken doors and through the double doors, then he's through the door to your immediate right."

Ryu took off into the air, where he bounced against the wall and flew with enough force to shatter through the double doors, then he found himself in the main room. He turned right and walked to a door, slammed his fist against it, and it splintered. Ryu heard a sigh behind him. "You know, they do open. You merely turn the handle."

Ryu ignored Leon and walked into the room, which was decorated in deep reds with a canopy bed, with Makoto resting in the middle. He walked over to him, crawled on the bed, and checked both sides of his neck.

"We generally don't feast on guests."

Ryu shot a glare at Leonhardt, who was leaning in the doorway. "Didn't stop you four years ago."

Leonhardt threw his hands in the air with an exasperated sigh. "Will you let that go? You did say, 'Bite me'...you invited me!"

Ryu growled as he got out of the bed. "I didn't mean it like that...it's an expression. Kind of like, 'fuck off,' and 'Eat shit and die.'" Ryu heard a snort from behind him and found Makoto slowly getting out of the bed.

"Actually, those are insults, Ryu."

Ryu smirked as he walked toward Makoto. "Are you all right?"

Makoto shrugged as he stood up. "Nothing a cup of tea and some sleep can't fix."

Ryu sighed as he looked Makoto over, who could barely

hold himself up. "All right you baka (Moron), come here." He threw Makoto's arm over his shoulder and led him to the door, where Leonhardt moved out of the way.

"Remember young one, we owe you. Call upon us when you require aid and we will be there on great wings of fury." Leonhardt bowed slightly as they passed.

Makoto nodded as Ryu led him to the door. "You're going to explain that to me later." Ryu jumped into the sky, taking Makoto with him as he laboriously headed home.

Chapter Four:
The Labyrinth of the Soul

Mamoru held his sword in front of him. "The part I'm holding is called the hilt, the point on the end is sharp." Ryu sighed as his sensei continued lecturing about the sword.

Takeo grinned as he saw Ryu slowly losing his patience. Finally Ryu growled angrily. "I know everything there is to know about swords Sensei; tell me why I'm here."

Mamoru grinned as he sheathed his blade. "It's simple. I've decided you two need to go over the basics while Makoto recovers, so we're starting at level zero." Ryu gritted his teeth before jumping into the air as his wings fanned out behind him, and he flew at his sensei with his sword drawn. Mamoru's grin fell as he pulled out his sword and blocked, while Ryu landed in a crouch and slashed up just as Mamoru slashed down.

Their swords met, sending sparks flying, but the sparks didn't fall; instead, they flared and flew up into Mamoru's eyes as Takeo attacked from the side. Mamoru flipped over Ryu before shoving him toward Takeo's attack. The duo grinned as Takeo grabbed Ryu's outstretched hand before spinning and throwing Ryu at Mamoru. Ryu slammed into their surprised sensei and knocked him to the ground with Ryu on top.

Ryu grinned as he held his sword to Mamoru's neck. "I

think we're past level zero, Sensei."

Mamoru shook his head before directing his eyes downward. Ryu followed his line of sight and found Mamoru's sword poised at his stomach. "Even if you cut my throat, I'll still gut you."

Ryu shook his head grimly. "So? If you did it wouldn't kill me."

Mamoru shook his head. "That's what we're doing this for. You can't keep throwing yourself in front of every attack or one of these times, it will kill you."

Ryu blinked before getting up. "Maybe death isn't so bad. Life's a bitch and then you die; why not skip the bitch and go straight to 'Go,' and forget the two hundred dollars?"

Mamoru straightened his back and glared. "You are Kami no densetsu no senshi-tachi. (The Legendary Warriors of the Gods.) You don't get the luxury of throwing in the towel."

Ryu growled as he rounded on his sensei. "Why? Who says we can't? We're at our peak. Our blades are silent, and I doubt they plan on saying shit any time soon."

Ryu blinked and the garden was gone. He was in the labyrinth again, but this time there was a white wisp coming from his chest that seemed to be a string leading down the hall. "What the hell? Why am I here again?"

He heard a small serene voice. It was calm, and the sound of it made all his hatred melt away, like it was never there. "Follow the wisp."

Ryu started walking, his feet carrying him as he stared down at the wisp he followed, his mind blank like he was on auto pilot; not once did he try to stop or turn around. He just followed the wisp. Finally, he came to a door and snapped out of his trance. The door was ordinary brown, and there was nothing to distinguish it from every other door around him. Ryu stared at it for a long time, his mind running in overdrive. What was that voice? Was it the thing from before? Could the thing even sound that...that... he couldn't think of a word that could describe the voice.

It was calm and serene and yet, there was an underlining howl of power, like the calm before the storm.

He grasped the handle of the door before slowly turning it, and when it wouldn't go anymore he stopped. What was the harm in opening a door? What could be in his own soul that was so terrifying that he couldn't fight it, couldn't destroy it? What part of him could be stronger then the conscious mind? The physical entity that was him?

He threw open the door and walked into the room slowly...the room was like a mausoleum. The ceiling had no apparent end, and hundreds upon hundreds of pillars were spaced far enough apart he and Takeo could walk side by side with the tips of their swords touching and their other arms outstretched, and they still wouldn't touch two pillars.

Each pillar had a torch on it, but even with all the light the room was still shrouded in darkness. "I've come. Now, where the hell am I?" His voice echoed far and he heard a noise like the scuffling of boots on the ground. He dashed behind a pillar and reached for his sword, only to find it gone. He was dressed in his morning yukata and was weaponless.

Why didn't I notice that earlier?

Suddenly the idea of walking into a room without his sword didn't sound so bright. He willed a sword into his hand, but nothing happened. So *much for that.*

Ryu was about to whirl around the pillar when he heard a voice. "Ryu?" Ryu's eyes widened as he looked around the pillar, and sure enough, standing there with a torch in his hand was Makoto.

Ryu walked out slowly. "Makoto? How the hell did you get here?"

Makoto's head shot toward him before he launched himself at Ryu. "Oh Kami-sama, I have no idea. I was resting in my bed, and then I woke up in this faded green labyrinth with all these doors and these crazy stairs. And this weird wisp string thing coming from my chest, and this odd feeling to follow it and it led me to this crazy cavern and then I heard your voice and I'm so glad. 'Cause this place creeps the hell out of me." Makoto started panting as he finished his explanation.

Ryu looked Makoto over to make sure nothing was wrong with him. "The same happened to me, except I woke up in this brown labyrinth. I wonder, if you and I are here, does that mean Takeo's somewhere in this nightmare?"

Makoto looked at him with fright. "You could be right, we have to find him."

Makoto grabbed his hand, and Ryu nodded slowly as they started walking. Ryu kept a close eye on Makoto, and every few minutes Ryu would call out for Takeo, but no answer would come back. Makoto was quiet, his eyes constantly ahead, his mouth closed and his breath calm and even. Finally, after what seemed like an eternity, Ryu growled. "All right, enough of this shit." He threw his hand at a pillar and a bolt of lightning shot from his palm, blasting a hole through six pillars before disappearing.

Makoto jumped with fright as he whirled around, a scowl on his face. "What the fuck are you doing?"

Ryu looked at him with a grin as he grabbed Makoto's throat and threw him. "Imposter! Makoto doesn't curse, and he doesn't scowl, and he sure as hell doesn't grab my hand." "Makoto" stood up, a grin on his face, before his body melted away to reveal a knight wearing black boots, that led up to a pair of black chain mail leggings, a sword at his waist with a gold hilt. A black chain mail shirt with a blood red cape was on his back, and his black gloves came together again and again, the sound loud in Ryu's ears.

His eyes focused on the small ridges of the gauntlets that were designed to make a single punch lethal. Finally, Ryu looked at his face. A black cowl with three white lines down the center made him stand out, but Ryu was focused on the acid green eyes and the red vapor that even now was smirking at him.

Ryu growled. "What the hell are you?"

The being shook his head. "I thought I was clear the last time we talked. I'm you, only better."

Ryu snorted; the voice, the face, everything about this thing was inhuman. "I thought that was a bad dream...seems like you're gonna be a pain in my ass after all."

The being's smirk widened. "Oh no, not at all. You see, I can't damage you too much. I still need you...or more accurately, I still need your body. You see, I'm gonna take your body and do what I want with it."

Ryu's eyes narrowed as he felt an all-consuming hatred. "You, Mamoru, Nobunaga. All you want is to control me." Lightning flashed around him as it came to his will. "I'm done being everyone's puppet. I'll kill you...I'll kill you all if that's what it takes to get my freedom." His voice was low, overflowing with malice, as the lightning formed in his hand, taking the shape of a sword.

The being only shook his head. "Don't worry, I'll have control, but I'll let you see everything. You can watch as I kill everyone; it'll be like you did it yourself."

The being nodded his head, the armor creaking, but Ryu wasn't listening. His mind was on the sword in his hand as it began to condense...first into his sword that he carried around, and then slowly it started to change, lengthen, and curve like a half moon. Ryu stayed focused on the blade as it curved around his body. He grabbed the hilt with both hands and held it up to his shoulder, where it curved all the way to his hip.

The being snorted, "Too late for that, brat." He drew his sword, a black katana that radiated evil. The being walked towards Ryu, the smirk never leaving his face. But Ryu was still focused on the sword he held in his own hand.

The lightning faded and he found himself mesmerized; the blade was stunning. It was black, then turned silver along the edge. He knew what this was; it was the soul of his sword. He felt stronger, and despite never wielding anything like it, he knew what he could do.

He swung the sword and it felt like an extension of himself, as if it was his own arm and not a heavy piece of metal. The blade swung in an arc before slamming into the ground, where a burst of energy erupted to fly off, a small blade of curved lightning. The attack smashed into the black knight and threw him into the darkness with a scream, then the cavern started to vanish and the sword with it. He found himself in the white room, and he wasn't alone.

He whirled around before stopping, stunned at what he saw. Before him, curled in the center of the room around the dais where his power orb had been, was a dragon with pure, glimmering silver scales. Its wings were folded around its body, its massive head looking at him with ruby red eyes. "Ryu, we meet at last."

Ryu would've bowed, but he found himself too shocked to move, think, or understand what he was seeing. The dragon raised its head and chuckled. "It's okay to speak, young one, I'm not your enemy."

Ryu nodded as he walked forward slowly. "Greetings. I'm Ryu, but you seem to know that. Which begs the question…who are you?"

The dragon shifted slightly. "I am, as you have guessed, the spirit of your sword."

Ryu nodded as he looked at the dais and there, bobbing up and down slowly, was the sword that he felt so in tune with.

"Do you know why not all swords have souls?"

Ryu was taken aback by this but nodded. "Yes, there are only twenty swords in existence that possess souls. Three held by my teammates and I, three by the Elders, and three by Mitsuo and his team. Right now the Elders are in possession of six unclaimed swords but five haven't been seen since the First War. They are a rare creation, and no one quite knows how they are created."

The dragon nodded. "Swords with souls, or Soul Swords, have been around for a long time, and are created by the Kami."

Ryu's eyes widened as the gravity of the blade he was carrying around hit him, and the dragon nodded again. "Yes, they are weapons created by the divine themselves. But it comes at a cost. While the weapon has immeasurable power, I'm sure you've asked yourself why they do and it's simple; Soul Swords are made when a Kami seals him or herself in their creation."

Ryu felt uneasy as he regarded the dragon before him with greater caution. "That means....."

The dragon nodded. "I am the Kami Raijin...you may call me Raiden. I have chosen this form to occupy the sword until the day of your death, at which point I will return to the care of the Kami until another suitable bearer can be found."

Ryu stumbled back and the dragon's tail whipped out to catch him before he fell. Ryu sat on the tail looking at the ground, white like the rest of the room, his mind overcome with everything. "That's not possible. I chose my sword from six others."

Raiden nodded. "Yes, you had a choice of Kami before you, but I spoke to you the loudest. That is why you chose me, and since you did, I am bound to you until your death."

Ryu looked at the ceiling. This was okay...life was okay. "So, Sensei wasn't joking when he said that I would unlock a power like no other."

Raiden chuckled and Ryu couldn't help but join in before his assailant moved to the front of his mind. "What was that thing that attacked me out there?"

Ryu looked at the door and Raiden sighed. "That was Tenma; he's the Oni I've had to share your soul with."

Ryu paled at the word "Demon." "Why's there a demon in my soul?"

Raiden grimaced with a nod. "Through the years, I've passed through many hands, and I'm afraid a little bit of my carrier's souls have stayed attached to the blade. Over the years that spirit has manifested itself, taking on the form of the first holder, and he began calling himself Tenma. Now he is trying desperately to take a human and use it as a vessel for his evil spirit, and I'm sorry to say, it has its eyes set on you."

Ryu shook his head, his eyes straying to the curved sword. "Why did it manifest now?"

Raiden could tell he didn't mean the sword. "He gains power from the evil in a person's soul. Unfortunately, I passed to you on the very cusp of his power, and he was able to take what little evil there was in you and become what you saw out there. I allowed you to summon my spirit to help, since he had stripped you of your weapon."

Ryu bowed at these words. "Thank you for your help; I wouldn't have stood a chance without your intervention."

Raiden shook his head. "No, the fight might have lasted longer, but I have little doubt you could've taken him without my assistance."

Ryu stood up and smiled sadly. "I'm glad so many people have faith in me, when I can't seem to find any."

Raiden stood up and walked to the other side of the room. "Maybe you're not looking in the right place, or you're looking for something that you think should be there but isn't yours to own." Raiden gave a small dragon smile. "But what do I know? I'm only an age old flying lizard. Grab the blade and you'll return to your body, and don't worry about Tenma. He may be able to take over in small bursts, but he has to kill you here to become the master of your body."

Ryu nodded. As he was about to grab the blade he remember something. "I heard a voice when I first came here. It was...well, it wasn't yours, or Tenma's."

The dragon lifted its head. "That may have been Fujin. I believe while you have been fighting your own personal demons, your friends have had an easier time finding and releasing their spirits."

Ryu snorted as he grabbed the blade. *Of course, they get the easy road while I have to fight uphill.* The white room vanished.

***

Ryu sat up; he was in his bed and it was dark out. He stood up and grabbed his sword from its place on the wall. He would have thought it a dream, but when he pulled his sword an inch from its sheathe, it wasn't normal. Once it had been a regular katana with no distinguishing marks, and now it looked like a straight version of his curved sword, black except for the edge that was silver. He placed the sword back and felt the increase in his power. It was like someone had opened a floodgate, and now all his power and strength that had been held back was pouring out. It felt like a tsunami, like all he had to do was let it sweep him away. But then that dream came back. *It could be a warning of what would happen if I did.* But even if the dream was right in that regard, it couldn't be right about Mitsuo. Why would he join with Mamoru? Maybe it was one of those instances where, "The enemy of my enemy is my friend."

He shook his head; life was getting complicated and irritating. "I need some air." He put his sword on and leapt out the window, jumping into the sakura tree just as the front door opened. Ryu looked down and saw Takeo and Makoto, both looking healthy with their swords in hand.

Good, glad to see nothing happened to them. Ryu leaned back, staring at the moon as it started to wane. The two on the ground walked over to the tree, and his white yukata helped him blend with the tree as they settled in. Ryu was content to let them talk, with him just a silent viewer.

Makoto sat down against the tree as Takeo joined him on the ground, both looking at the moon. "That was something."

Takeo snorted as he placed his sword in his lap. "Something? That was the single most defining thing that has ever and probably will ever happen! I mean, our swords are the vessels of gods. Mako, gods."

Makoto nodded as he too placed his sword in his lap. "I can hear her. Can you?"

Takeo looked down at his sword, shaking his head. "Not yours, but mine yes. Bishamonten, the god of war." Takeo shook his head, chuckling. "The god of war! Can you believe it?"

Makoto pulled out his sword; it was like Ryu's, only with green instead of black. "She's beautiful. Fujin, the goddess of the wind."

Takeo shrugged as he pulled out his sword, red instead of green. "Yeah, I always thought Fujin was a god."

Makoto shook his head as he sheathed his sword. "No, turns out with the Kami, they're not bound by sex or form. Fujin was male before she came into my possession. The Kami will take a form that closely matches its wielder's spirit."

Takeo sniggered as he looked at Makoto, wiggling his eyebrows. "Your spirit is like that of a female."

Makoto blushed as he turned away from Takeo. "Shut up, jerk wad."

Takeo laughed as he rested against the tree. "It's so funny how you refuse to cuss; only another example that you have a chick's spirit."

Makoto smacked him upside the head and he laughed harder. "Only proving my point." He rolled away from Makoto's lunge and ran away, Makoto giving chase, both leaving their swords next to the tree.

Ryu smiled. They were killers, thieves, whatever whoever needed them to be. But when it was just them, they were human, barely out of the cusp of childhood, and they could still laugh, still play like children. Maybe it was because they had to grow up too fast. They didn't get to play, and in these moments they were just catching up on lost time. Ryu didn't know, but maybe there was hope for them;

maybe all they really needed was each other. Ryu dropped from the tree and sat down with the other swords, Takeo's on his right and Makoto's on his left. He placed his sword on the ground and let it lean on his shoulder as he watched the other two play.

Chapter Five:
Past Foes, Present Dangers

Mamoru smiled as he watched his students play in the yard like children, and Ryu their ever-watchful guardian. Mamoru suddenly bent over, coughing. He covered his mouth to stifle the sound, but before long he was on his knees, blood dripping from between his fingers. He pulled his hand away from his mouth and stared at the blood as it slowly dripped to the floor.

"It's getting worse," he sighed as he walked to the counter, his breath returning slowly. "Won't be long now." He shook his head as he cleaned the blood from his hand and then went back for the blood on the floor. "I wonder if they can survive without me?" He mused while he dabbed at the blood on the floor. Experience told him this was the most effective way to clean up spilled blood.

He stood up, the cloth vanishing into the folds of his robes, and smiled again; just seeing his students relax enough to play was comforting. The only one who wouldn't relax was Ryu, always alert, always on guard, rarely if ever sparing a smile, unless it was to put Makoto at ease. "Ah, how the years have come and gone."

***

Ten years earlier.

87

Mamoru walked up the stairs toward the council chambers, his student next to him. He was wearing a formal outfit for the meeting like his sensei, his short silver hair and easygoing face giving him the appearance of age. But he really was just leaving his childhood behind. "Sensei, do you know why the Elders summoned you?"

Mamoru shook his head, his short sandy blond hair moving back and forth. "No Zenaku, I have not the faintest idea."

Zenaku snorted as they approached the top of the stairs, where a guard in red stopped them. Mamoru stopped before the guard, a light smile on his face. "Mamoru and Zenaku Hattori to see the council."

The guard shook his head at Zenaku. "You may enter, but your protégé must wait here. Lord Nobunaga's orders."

Zenaku shrugged as he leaned against a pillar next to the door. "It's all good, Sensei. You know how the council is; they just fear my awesome power."

Mamoru chuckled as he walked through the doors and into the chamber beyond. He walked down the long cavern-like room to the three thrones before dropping to one knee, his head bowed and his right arm crossed over his heart.

"You summoned me, my lords?" He heard the sound of shifting armor.

"Mamoru Hattori, rise."

Mamoru rose, his head held high. "What can I humbly do for you?"

Nobunaga gave a bloodthirsty grin. "We have a job for you."

Mamoru cocked his head. "With all due respect, I don't see why this couldn't have been explained in a scroll."

Nobunaga turned toward a door on the far side of the room, and to Mamoru's surprise, a guard was leading three children towards them. As soon as they stood before the council, the guard bowed and left, leaving the children standing before the adults. They were small, appearing to be about eight years in age. One with forest green hair was sniffling and looked to be on the verge of tears, while a boy with dark red hair tried to comfort him. The last, with dark blue hair, stayed away from the other two, and glared at everything with a hatred that no child should know.

"Makoto Tokugawa, Takeo Toyotomi, and Ryu Oda."

Mamoru turned toward Nobunaga, a look of shock clear on his face.

"The Elder clans were destroyed from within; I'm sure you've heard."

Mamoru nodded mutely as he stared at the children again. "These are the ones that inherited the Power?"

Nobunaga nodded, his smirk still in place. "We want you to train them."

Mamoru shook his head as his eyes shot back toward Nobunaga. "I can't; I have a student of my own. I don't have the time."

Nobunaga chuckled, and the dark sound of it made the hairs on the back of Mamoru's neck stand on end. "Student? Not anymore you don't; or at least you won't when you leave here. Is that understood?"

Mamoru gritted his teeth, knowing exactly what Nobunaga meant. Mamoru gave a brisk bow. "Yes, Lord Nobunaga."

He stood up and something caught his eye. He turned towards Ryu and looked down at his right hand, now noticing the skin was blackened and pulsing. "Lord Nobunaga, his hand...."

Nobunaga sat back down, his armor barely rattling as his face became neutral. "Yes, demonic possession. Unnerving, isn't it?"

Mamoru looked at the boy with greater caution. "What do you want me to do about that?"

Nobunaga smirked again. "Nothing. If it manifests, let it. If it doesn't, don't provoke it. We are eager to see what will happen." He gestured at the empty thrones. "Now go.

The children will be brought by as soon as your student...retires."

Mamoru's mind snapped back to what he was supposed to do. He bowed and left without a word, and only a single glance at the children. Ryu's eyes never left his...never blinked, as if he was challenging Mamoru.

Mamoru walked out the doors; the suffocating air of the cavern had left him with a greater need for fresh air than he realized.

Zenaku greeted him with a grin. "So, what did the old codgers want, Sensei?"

Mamoru felt his heart clench as he walked past his student and down the steps. Zenaku followed with a bewildered look on his face.

"Was it so bad you can't tell me, Sensei?"

Mamoru still didn't respond and Zenaku took this as a bad sign.

"Or was it just top secret? If it is, just nod and I'll let it go, Sensei."

Mamoru whirled on him and rammed his fist into Zenaku's stomach. The boy fell to the ground, coughing and holding his gut, in obvious pain. Mamoru looked down at him, mustering up a disgusted glare.

"I'm no longer your sensei." He turned and continued walking, hoping against everything that Zenaku would let it drop and just leave. But he'd known the boy long enough to know that he wouldn't let it go...he never did.

"Hey, wait; what the hell was that for?" Zenaku appeared in front of him with a glare, one arm crossed over his stomach with a grimace.

Mamoru remained cold as he glared. "You heard me. I am no longer your sensei. I have better things to do then train a weakling."

Zenaku stumbled back like Mamoru had hit him again. "W-what Sensei? What's wrong? Is this part of the mission?"

Mamoru prayed his student would dodge and pulled his blade with a horizontal slash. Like Mamoru had taught him, Zenaku leaped back as he drew his own blade, and held it in front of him in a two handed grip. "Sensei! What the hell is wrong with you? You could've killed me."

Mamoru snorted as he mimicked Zenaku's pose. "Good riddance; one less waste of space." Mamoru had a thought and relaxed. "But I won't kill you...you're not worth staining my blade over. Instead, I'll leave you here with no way to return."

Zenaku opened his mouth, but was silenced when Mamoru slammed into him with a vicious kick that sent him flying down the steps. Mamoru calmly but quickly slashed the air and cut a portal to his home. He had set one foot through when he heard Zenaku cry out. "Sensei! You can't leave me here, it's not right!"

Mamoru looked over his shoulder, and what he saw almost made him run to his student. Zenaku was clutching a wound on his upper arm, and judging by the blood on Zenaku's blade, it must have happened when he fell.

Zenaku glared up at Mamoru. "It's not fair! I've done nothing wrong! Why are you doing this?"

Mamoru shook his head while he chuckled cruelly. "Life isn't fair. Consider this extreme training. If you survive you might be worthy to stand in my presence again."

Mamoru continued forward but hesitated, and this gave Zenaku the opportunity to launch forward and strike Mamoru in the small of his back. Mamoru fell forward as the portal collapsed, Zenaku's last whispered words before he struck Mamoru running through his head. "Dim Mok (Death Touch)."

Mamoru fell into his kitchen as anger bubbled up in his stomach before fading. "I would've done the same if someone destroyed my life like that."

***

Mamoru snapped back to the present, his tea cold in his

91

hands as the door opened. Ryu walked through alone, took one look at Mamoru, and asked, "What's wrong, Sensei?"

Mamoru smiled as he relaxed. "Nothing Ryu…just happy to see that the three of you are alright."

Ryu nodded slowly as if considering whether to challenge his words, but then sat down and poured himself a glass of tea. "Sensei, you would tell me if something was wrong, right?"

Mamoru hesitated before he nodded. "Of course Ryu, I have nothing to hide."

Ryu's eyes narrowed before the door opened and the others walked in. Makoto looked around before his eyes landed on Ryu.

"Ryu! You're okay!" Makoto walked toward him but stayed two feet away.

Ryu looked away from Mamoru's face and turned his gaze toward Makoto. "Yes Makoto, I'm fine."

Takeo was next to Makoto with a grin on his face. "You know, if you're gonna try and die on us, don't make some last minute recovery for the attention. OW!"

Makoto whacked him on the head with a glare. "Be nice, Ryu's been through a lot."

Ryu grinned as he stood up. "Yeah, I've been through a lot, so piss off Takeo." Ryu looked over his shoulder at Mamoru, who just smiled and refused to speak. Ryu's eyes caught sight of a trace of blood on his sensei's sleeve before he walked toward the door.

"Where are you going Ryu?" Makoto looked at Ryu's retreating form, but Ryu didn't give him an answer. Instead, he walked out the door and closed it behind him.

Mamoru looked at the closed door with a slight grimace. "Never mind him Makoto; Ryu's just working through some things."

***

Ryu walked away from the house, toward the back and into the forest beyond. His eyes focused on his hand, but his

92

mind was wandering. *Blood, but Sensei hasn't been near it in days and that was fresh. Plus, the scent was in the air; he bled sometime before I walked in and after I left through my window. But he wouldn't accidentally cut himself...he's too careful for that. He couldn't have done it intentionally; so then, where did the blood come from?*

His thoughts shifted back to the kitchen, where a small red spot at the corner of his sensei's mouth had caught his gaze. *Is he sick? If he is and it's serious enough to make him cough blood, why wouldn't he tell us?*

Ryu lashed out, slamming his fist into a tree with a cry of frustration. The tree bowed lightly before righting itself. He leaned against the tree and slid to the ground. *It can't be an illness...he can't get sick. It must have been an attack of some kind. But Sensei hasn't been in a fight since he started training us...so it must be something that happened awhile ago. But what?*

Ryu's mind started to wander over everything he could think of, from elemental attacks to weapons, something that could cause a lingering effect. Something moved at the edge of his memory, an obscure text he had once read in his home. The name had just started to form when he heard something snap to his left.

Ryu jumped to his feet with his sword in hand. "Who goes there?" He was met with silence and his eyes could see no movement, but he knew he heard something snap, a branch or a twig. It was something, not a memory.

"Show yourself!" He shouted into the darkness, but again silence was his only answer. He started backing toward the house that was well over five hundred feet behind him, but he didn't dare turn around and run.

The silence coupled with the darkness was enough that he felt the need to call on his sword. "Raiden, come to me." In a flash, the half moon formed, already settling him and making him feel whole.

At this, he heard a chuckle. "Tsk, tsk. The little boy has

awakened his sword; how cute." A man dropped out of the trees, a grin on his face as he brandished his sword. The man was six feet tall, his shoulders broad and strong. His long silver hair was tied behind his head, and he wore a black shinobi shozoku without the cowl. He had dark green eyes that radiated hatred.

"I am Zenaku Hattori, and I've come for what you took from me."

Ryu relaxed slightly at his name before he fell into a battle stance. "Hattori, you share the name of my sensei."

Zenaku chuckled as he walked forward. "Yes; he wasn't always your sensei, now was he?"

Ryu opened his mouth but didn't have the chance to speak before Zenaku attacked. Ryu jumped to the side and Zenaku's blade slashed through the tree behind him. Zenaku kicked the base and watched as it fell on Ryu, who had barely recovered when the trunk slammed on his arm, pinning him to the ground. Ryu cried out as his arm shattered under the weight, only for his arm to heal and shatter again, leaving him to writhe in agony as his body attempted to fix the damage but was only making it worse.

Zenaku sat on the tree trunk and watched while Ryu suffered. "I know all about your ability to regenerate; it's involuntary, right? Which means your body is going to continue to heal that arm until your power exhausts itself." Ryu could feel his sword grasped in his right hand, but he knew he was powerless as long as his arm was pinned. Then he had an idea. He raised his left arm to the sky as Zenaku threw his head back and laughed, the situation too funny for him to handle. Lightning clouds formed overhead before a single bolt struck into Ryu's open palm. Zenaku looked down a second too late.

"RAI KEN!" Ryu slammed his fist into the tree and let the power go. Zenaku jumped away, covering his face as the tree exploded, sending splinters of wood zooming away like small projectiles.

Zenaku lowered his hands and smirked at what he saw. Ryu was slowly standing, but his entire right arm had blackened, along with the right side of his torso. Red spider veins spanned his torso and seemed to burn through the cloth, until his shirt was tattered enough to slip from his shoulders. Black eyes were focused on Zenaku with a sightless stare.

Zenaku straightened slowly, and even then Ryu's eyes followed. "Well, this is an interesting development. Who do I have the honor of meeting?"

Ryu blinked as he straightened. "Tenma; you may call me Tenma."

Zenaku grinned as Tenma effortlessly kicked away the remainder of the tree and picked up his blade. Zenaku watched as the crescent shape exploded as it turned into a black katana.

Tenma aimed the blade at Zenaku. "Friend or foe?"

Zenaku bowed slightly as he backed away. "Friend, or at least not your foe. I merely want to kill your vessel."

Tenma nodded before he slid into a battle stance. "That makes you a foe." He wasted no other words before he attacked, disappearing and reappearing behind Zenaku with a horizontal slash. But the attack was easily blocked before Zenaku jumped away, flipping in mid air to face Tenma as he fell.

"I didn't plan for this…hmm. I suppose I'll just kill you both." They battled back and forth, destroying huge swathes of the forest around them, but neither could gain ground. As time went on, Tenma was losing control as Ryu was fighting his way back to the forefront of his mind.

"Idiot! I'm trying to save your life!"

Ryu growled as he slowly ripped control back, and Zenaku could see the change. Ryu's attacks became less about brute force and more about speed, slashing faster and faster. The veins had started to recede, until finally the only thing that still showed any signs of possession was his right hand. As soon as the veins had reached his wrist, his sword exploded and curved.

One attack slipped through and cut Zenaku along his torso. *How can he move between styles like that?*

Ryu kept attacking, his sword held in a loose grip to allow the greatest range of movement. Finally, Zenaku was forced to jump back and take a breather, while Ryu panted before he threw his sword at Zenaku, which forced him to leap into the air well over the trees.

Ryu smirked as he threw his hand up and another Rai Ken struck. He ran forward and went under Zenaku before he rebounded off a tree, leaping into the air, and ran his fist through Zenaku's back, causing blood to rain down. "Never jump into the air, it leaves you defenseless."

But something was setting off Ryu's internal alarms. Why wasn't Zenaku screaming? In fact, he was perfectly still.

Zenaku looked over his shoulder, an insane smirk on his face. "Never get to close to an opponent; it leaves you open for an attack that you can't counter against." He was suddenly behind Ryu faster than Ryu could follow. He locked Ryu's arms behind his back and kicked him in the shin with enough force to alter their trajectory and send them both diving head first into the ground. Ryu struggled as Zenaku ducked down, and a wave of horror went through Ryu as he realized what was about to happen.

Zenaku was going to let him slam head first into the ground…there would be no way that he could regenerate from that. He looked at the ground as it raced faster and faster toward them. He constantly tried to wiggle free, but Zenaku had him in a vice grip he couldn't break. He growled and fought, but there was no way he could get out of it.

"Good bye bastard."

Ryu felt Zenaku let go six feet from the ground, but there was no way Ryu could right himself in time. He slammed into the ground and felt the force of the impact roll through him, cracking, splintering, and shattering his bones. He looked up at the sky as an immeasurable amount of pain ripped through his body. Ryu knew he was bleeding...he could feel it surrounding him. Zenaku walked into his view with a grin on his face. He said something, but Ryu couldn't hear it.

The sound of his bones echoed in his ears.... The horrific sound was the only thing he could hear. Only his ability to read lips let him know Zenaku's last words to a dying man.

"One down, two to go."

Ryu watched as Zenaku walked off, rain starting to pour from the sky. He could hear his heartbeat pumping faster than it should, and he felt the pain. But it was like he was sitting in the back seat to someone else's pain. Then he felt his heart start to stop; first it was barely perceptible, then it stuttered, then stopped altogether, and Ryu's world went black.

***

Takeo watched as Makoto paced back and forth like a caged animal. Mamoru was looking out the window as rain pelted the glass.

Makoto kept shooting glances at the door. "I'm telling you, something's not right; he should've been back by now."

Takeo rolled his eyes. "Please, Makoto, chill. He's probably out there enjoying the rain. He'll be back when he's done thinking, or when he gets hungry."

Mamoru looked out the corner of his eye at the door; truth be told, he was worried. He thought he had seen the Rai Ken, but he couldn't be sure. *No, there's no chance. No one knows where to find us; our location is one of the most carefully guarded secrets in the ninja hierarchy.* And it was...almost no one knew where they were. The only ones who knew the location of his house were the Elders, and only then because they had erected the barrier. Besides them there was one messenger that delivered their missions—and he was sworn under so many blood oaths, there would be no way for him to reveal their location even if he died.

There's no chance, none at all...but still. Mamoru stood up. The sudden movement had stopped whatever argument the others had been having because they turned to him.

"Sensei?"

Mamoru turned to them as they spoke. "Makoto, head south. Keep yourself out of sight and look for traces of him. Takeo, take the east...same goes for you. I'll head west. He wouldn't have gone north; that would only take him to the sea, and we all know he hates the smell of salt water." His students were out the door after he gave his orders. They had only seen him in full sensei-mode once, and that had been what saved Makoto from losing his head in an ambush.

Mamoru was the last out the door, and he saw that his students were mere specks on the horizon. He had intentionally sent them in the wrong directions so that they wouldn't come upon the scene he feared he would find.

Mamoru ran full out, heading into the forest behind the house. He ran faster than he knew he could, fear and adrenalin pushing him beyond the normal limitations of his body. Then his fears were realized as he saw evidence of a battle...trees knocked over, broken and scorched ground. "Kami-sama no. RYU!" He hollered Ryu's name, hoping, if nothing else, he would hear something, anything...some sound that said he still had a chance. He ran in large arcs around the clearing, yelling, "RYU!" But still no sound came back.

He turned, and fell to his knees at what lay before him.

Ryu's body was broken. Bits of white poked out of the skin, and blood pooled around him before being washed away by the rain. Mamoru stumbled to his feet, tears streaming down his face. "Ryu, oh kami Ryu. No! Please no!" His voice was broken as he fell to his knees next to Ryu's head. His neck was twisted and bent at an angle, his skull was cracked open, and there were tinges of gray on the forest floor. His limbs were entirely turned around, the bones sticking out like a demented pin cushion. Ryu's body was bent almost far enough for his ankles to touch his shoulders. Mamoru reached out with shaking hands and touched his face, which was littered with cuts. Ryu stared straight up with glassy, filmed eyes, and Mamoru knew there was no chance he was alive. He threw back his head and howled at the heavens as the sea, five hundred feet away, turned treacherous and started roiling end over end.

Chapter Six:

The Broken Sword of the Gods

Ryu opened his eyes and blinked as he stood up. He looked down at himself and saw he was wrapped in a white robe; no blood or bones sticking out. He looked around and found the walls were black. Ryu walked over to them and cocked his head at himself. *Must be black marble.* He clicked his tongue as he turned toward the only door in his line of sight. His eyes wandered over the walls and found no windows or torches, but he had more than sufficient light. He walked toward the door and it slid open as he approached. His feet carried him through the door and he found himself in a hallway made of the same black marble. He looked to the left and the right, but didn't see any people or doors, so he started down the right path.

"When in doubt, right is always *right*," he mused to himself as he continued walking. His feet made no sound, no matter how hard he stomped. A thought went through his head; he couldn't hear Raiden, he had no blade, and yet he felt content...like he could walk forever and be perfectly happy. Ryu forcefully shook his head at this absurd thought as his footsteps became lighter and faster, his training kicking in faster than he could react. But it was natural and he knew what he had to do. *Sword, appropriate clothes, and then a way out.* He slipped down hallway after hallway, not knowing which way was back or forward...everything was the same. Getting frustrated he started zigzagging, left then right, then left again, hoping for something to appear.

Then he caught sight of something—a sword's sheathe—that disappeared down a path on the left. He was quick to follow and came upon a man with wild blue hair who was dressed in a blue green yukata. His right hand was resting on the hilt of a katana as he walked. Ryu could feel the power that poured from this man as he snuck up behind him, his every move silent as he reached for the man's sword. But at the last second the man dashed away from him before spinning around and drawing his blade.

He glared at Ryu, his lightning blue eyes dancing with power. "My sister saves you and you have the audacity to try and steal off me; mortals are all the same." His voice was low and calm, yet it felt like he was screaming. Ryu slid away into a defensive stance, glancing around. There was no way he could use the Rai Ken in the halls, he didn't have a sword, and he was facing a pissed off opponent. The man charged and Ryu reacted on instinct...he thrust his palm forward and a lightning bolt shot from his hand and struck the man in the chest, throwing him down the hall with the greatest force Ryu had ever seen from that attack. Normally the power of lightning that he called from within was weaker, which was why he always relied on the natural elements.

Ryu stared down at his palm in shock. *Somehow this place is augmenting my powers. Which means....* He placed his palm facing the ground, and instead of shooting a bolt of lightning, his fist was enveloped in a perfect shimmering blade.

Ryu grinned as the man came at him again. His blue katana slammed into Ryu's arm, but couldn't cut through it.

Ryu's grin turned vicious as he threw the man back before launching forward and stabbing him in the chest. A laugh started to bubble in his chest before it spilled over, starting as a small chuckle, and before long he was stabbing the man in the chest over and over with his right hand while he held him aloft with his left. His laughter had become full blow hysterics. "HAHAHAHAHA!" He was lost to the power, and as his own death played over and over in his head, his mind started to splinter and crack.

Suddenly he heard a voice speak from behind him. "Enough." It was calm and steady, the things Ryu himself didn't feel, and he did stop.

"Release him."

His left hand opened and dropped the man, who fell to his knees coughing as he glared past the owner of the voice to a man who stood back a ways, dressed in black leathers like an ancient highwayman. He had an amused look on his face, while he brushed bone white hair out of his face. "That wasn't cool, Tsukiyomi."

The man on the ground stood up and waved his hand over the damage Ryu had done, which disappeared like it had never been there. He walked past Ryu, who was still frozen.

"No, but it was fun, Susanoo." Tsukiyomi's voice was the epitome of calm, as if he couldn't be fazed. Ryu fell to his knee. The murderous rage had left him, and he rolled to his feet to regard the three before him, his eyes focused on the only female of the group. She had long fiery red hair and a serene smile on her face. She wore an extravagant dress that wouldn't be ready for battle in a million years, but Ryu felt, even if she was his sole enemy, he couldn't bring himself to attack her.

"Who are you three?" He felt he knew the answer, but needed to hear it from their own lips.

"I am Amaterasu, my brother Tsukiyomi, and that delinquent would be Susanoo."

Ryu growled as he stood up. Susanoo had a smug look on his face before Ryu flew across the hall and grabbed him. Ryu whirled him around with a growl before letting go and launching him at Tsukiyomi, and they both flew into the wall. He rounded on Amaterasu, rage pouring off him like a poison as he looked her in the eyes.

"What right do you have to choose our fates? What gives you the right to say who we are? Who we can be? And who we can be with? You don't have the fucking right!"

Lightning raced off him and gouged deep lines into the grounds and walls as Amaterasu stood in the middle of the hall. Ryu was panting. He felt such anger, such hatred, the likes of which scared him, but he knew without it he wouldn't have what it took to challenge the Kami themselves.

Amaterasu smiled as she walked forward. "Do you hate us so much, really?"

Ryu nodded curtly. He heard shuffling behind him as Tsukiyomi restrained Susanoo. "With every fiber of my being, I despise you; if I had the power, I'd kill you." Ryu glared at her as she touched him, and he felt a deep calm wash over him.

"This anger is not yours. It comes from the demon with which you share your soul. As this place makes you stronger, it also makes him stronger. You have to fight harder to contain him, and he has to fight harder to obtain his freedom."

She took her hand away and he felt all of his rage come back; his glare was now focused on her hands, making sure to keep them in his view at all times. Ryu took a step back, his eyes never straying from her hands. "I've felt this hatred towards the Kami since before I can remember."

Amaterasu smiled sadly as she looked over his shoulder. "Brother, will you please try to talk some sense into him?"

He heard Tsukiyomi approach behind him and a hand fell on his shoulder. He grabbed the appendage and threw the Kami over his body and down the hall. "I don't need someone to tell me what's wrong. It's you, always you!" He harnessed the lightning and formed it into a blast of power that he threw at Tsukiyomi; the attack filled the hallway, enveloped the Kami, and blasted through wall after wall. "I will not calm down...I'll kill you all!"

Susanoo was sneaking up behind him, and he grabbed him and slammed him into the wall, then started pounding his fists into the blue haired man's stomach. Ryu reveled in the sound as he punched harder and faster. His fists turned into a blur, and he could feel the shock wave move up and down his arms, but he couldn't stop. He wanted the Kami pulverized, destroyed, and ultimately he wanted to accomplish what no one else had...he wanted to kill a god.

Amaterasu appeared beside him as he laid into Susanoo. "Do you really want to continue feeling this anger? Wouldn't you rather feel like you used to, happy and content with the world? Wasn't it easier before the rage?"

Ryu stopped. Susanoo was embedded into the wall and was unable to fall forward, but this time he showed no sign of pain, like he didn't even feel Ryu's fists. He shook his head at Amaterasu. "Quit trying to help him...you can't fix a man who wants to stay broken."

Ryu stepped away from Susanoo as the god disappeared and reappeared next to Tsukiyomi, who didn't look any worse for wear. Ryu still felt anger, still felt the need to put his fist through something, but Susanoo had struck a cord in him. "'Stay broken.'" Was that what he was? A broken man? Was that why Mamoru always handled him with care, like he was glass? *No. Makoto's the tender one, the innocent one. Not me...I'm the sword. I'm the weapon of the three. I'm the first line against all the evil in the world. I...I...I am broken! I am the broken sword of the Kami. That's why I haven't been able to beat Mitsuo, I'm damaged. I should be stronger but I'm not, and this...this makes sense. The reason I'm not at the power level I should be is because I've lost my edge. No, it's not that I lost it...I've never found my edge.*

Ryu looked up, his eyes clouded as he turned to Amaterasu. "How?"

She smiled at him and gestured for him to follow, which Ryu did numbly as she led him down more halls till they came to a door. Like the room he had awoken in, the doors slid open as they approached, and they entered. "This is the armory."

Ryu looked around. Sacred and mythical weapons were everywhere, but there was one that he focused on, one he had often fantasized about having in his youth. She led him to it and gently pulled it from the rack where it rested. "The Kusanagi. Susanoo pulled it from the body of the eight headed snake Orochi...I now pass it to you." She held it out to him with it resting in the palms of her hands.

Ryu recoiled from it. "I can't accept it."

She smiled and pushed her hands toward him. "Please, consider this the Kami's way of trying to make up for a mistake we made."

Ryu placed his hands close together and slid them under the blade before he lifted it from her grasp, then bowed over it and touched his brow to it. "I humbly accept this gift."

Amaterasu continued smiling. "And we, the Kami, humbly give it in the hopes that it will help right a wrong."

Ryu felt the rage falling into him before being locked in a cage far from his conscious. "I have never heard of the Kusanagi's ability to do that."

Amaterasu nodded as she swept her hand over the sheath. "Yes, there are a great many things that the world doesn't know about our sacred weapons. Kusanagi has the power to seal evil deep within a person, but you must know it is still there. I could vanquish the demon from you, but I'm afraid even the Kami must heed the hand of Fate, and the demon is a part of your Fate."

Ryu tucked the sword into the belt of his robe. "What is my fate?"

Amaterasu's smile turned sad. "I can't tell you." Ryu nodded, finding that since the anger was gone he could think rationally again. "I could tell you, but it would be pointless as you will forget everything you have seen since you awakened as soon as we send you back."

Ryu stepped back as he regarded the being before him. "Send me back?"

Amaterasu nodded, her happy smile back. "Yes, we still need you down there."

Ryu was happy beyond belief. "Why will I forget?"

Amaterasu laughed, the sound like nothing he had ever heard. "We can't very well send you back after everything you've seen and done; your mortal mind wouldn't be able to take it...not now. But one day we will return the memory of your time."

Ryu nodded with a smile of his own. He felt happier now than he had in a long time. Then a thought occurred to him that derailed his good mood. "But, my body was—"

Amaterasu waved her hand with a smile. "Never you mind that. We'll make it like it never happened. You'll be whole and happy, and you'll take the sword with you, which will be the only thing you take." Ryu nodded as she looked him over.

"Well, I do believe you are ready to go." Ryu nodded and Amaterasu placed her palm against his head. The world exploded before his eyes as Amaterasu's voice guided him back to his body.

"We can't send you back to your dimension. But we can send you to a dimension close by; how you get back is up to you." Then he fell.

Chapter Seven:
Time of Mourning

Mamoru had fixed the body as well as he could; the blood had stopped running a long time ago. But the tears still hadn't stopped, nor had the rain. *Why Ryu? He was young, he still had so much to experience.*

Mamoru picked Ryu's sword up and tucked it into his own waistband before he gently picked up the body, hooking his right arm under Ryu's neck and the other under his legs, and started to head home. He knew what he would have to do. *I'm going to have to bury one of my students.*

No more than a second after the thought crossed his mind he suddenly found that he wanted to curl up and let go, but the thought of his remaining students was enough to keep him going, enough to keep him walking. He didn't know how to break the news to Makoto and Takeo...he hoped he wouldn't have to.

He hated himself, but he hoped they were there when he walked through so he wouldn't have to tell them when they came back...he knew he didn't have the heart to do it. He wanted to tell his students how Ryu had died valiantly, but the truth was he had no idea, and he doubted that the one who did it would ever come forward. His house came into view and he'd never hated it more.

He glanced down at Ryu's still face. He had closed the

eyes, not being able to stand staring into the lifeless eyes any longer. Back when he had been a field operative he had reveled in looking into the lifeless eyes of his enemies, but when it was a comrade—or in this case someone he considered to be his own son—he couldn't stand it.

He was at the front door, and could hear Takeo and Makoto inside arguing over whether or not to go looking for their missing comrades. They silenced as he opened the door, and Takeo was on his feet after rising from the couch. "Sensei, did you...?" He trailed off, seeing Ryu clutched in his arms.

Makoto approached slowly. "Is he okay?" Mamoru walked past them and laid the body on the counter. He stumbled back, away from his students, as Takeo checked for a pulse, and a look of utter disbelief crossed his face. "No! It's not possible." Makoto had started to cry as Takeo checked and rechecked, but he still couldn't find a pulse. "No! This isn't happening! He's playing a bad joke on us! Hey Ryu? Wake up! You got us man...very funny. WAKE UP!"

Makoto started to shake the body, but stopped as soon as he heard the bones underneath the skin scraping together. Makoto fell to the floor, tears streaming down his face, constantly mumbling. "No. No." He started to rock, but Takeo couldn't take his eyes off the body.

"Please Ryu! I was joking! Make a last minute recovery, I don't mind, I was only joking! Please Ryu!" But Ryu wasn't playing in any sense of the word, and Takeo slowly resigned himself to the fact that Ryu was well and truly gone. He shot a glare at Mamoru.

"Were you there when it happened?"

Mamoru slowly shook his head and Makoto cried harder as he stumbled to his feet to lean on the counter.

"He died alone?" Takeo's voice broke as he gently righted the body.

Mamoru hated how his head jerked slightly as he

nodded. "I found him dead."

Makoto cried over the body as Takeo walked to the door and out. He was furious, Mamoru could tell, because the rain evaporated before it even touched him. Mamoru heard a scream as intense heat enveloped the house. Makoto looked out the window and found Takeo standing in the middle of a raging inferno that was slowly but surely glassing the area around him. He had fallen to his knees with his hands balled up in front of him.

Mamoru pulled water from the ocean and dropped it on Takeo, who gave a hiss as his fire was doused. Mamoru was on the porch, a glare on his face. "This is not behavior befitting a ninja."

Takeo rose from the ground and walked toward him, neither noticing that the rain had stopped. "Screw behavior; Ryu's DEAD! He's fucking dead, none of it matters anymore." Takeo was standing in front of Mamoru and had no time to react before Mamoru backhanded him.

"Don't speak like that near his body; he gave everything for this life. Even if he's dead, do you think he would want you to talk like this?"

Takeo growled but backed away with a grimace. "No, he'd kick my ass for even thinking like that."

Mamoru nodded as he walked back in the house to find Makoto still crying over the body. Mamoru walked over and placed his hand on Makoto's shoulder. "It's okay." Makoto whirled around and Mamoru held him while he cried.

Takeo came up beside them and gazed at Makoto with pity. "What do we do now?"

Mamoru looked at the body. Besides the red marks on the skin and the state of his clothes, Mamoru would almost say Ryu was peacefully sleeping. "We have to lay the body to rest."

Takeo nodded and Makoto cried harder. Mamoru gestured to a closet that led into the basement. "I have a coffin down there that we can use." Takeo looked at his sensei, who smiled sadly. "I had always intended for it to be used for my body someday, but I think it would be okay for Ryu."

Takeo was gone in a flash as Mamoru gently pried Makoto off him. "We should find a place to bury him." Makoto nodded and Mamoru led them outside.

Makoto walked around before he pointed to a spot under the sakura tree. "He used to sit there a lot." Mamoru smiled as he gestured for Makoto to move. "How are you gonna dig the hole?"

Mamoru smiled sadly as he focused. "My primary element is water, but I have a little bit of control over earth." At his command the earth started to shake as a seven by four foot slab started to lift itself from the ground. The slab rose six feet before Mamoru set it to the side. He was panting but it was done.

"Not bad, Sensei." Takeo laid a plain coffin next to his sensei as he spoke, his voice barely above a whisper.

Mamoru looked at Takeo and found him on the verge of tears. "I'm sorry, Takeo."

Takeo shook his head as his throat closed on itself. "I'm not the one who's dead, Sensei." His voice was small and broken, but Mamoru knew he refused to ask for comfort like Makoto could. So Mamoru looked at him, the question clear in his eyes.

"I'm good Sensei, just...this doesn't feel real." He walked back toward the house and Mamoru followed shortly after.

Mamoru found Takeo sitting next to the body. "Don't you worry about a thing Ryu. I'll look after Makoto...I'll keep our family safe. I'm sure that's how you died, keeping us safe." He bowed his head over the body and tears slid down his face. "I'll grow strong enough for us both Ryu, I swear." He stood up as Mamoru walked in.

"We'll bury him in what he's wearing, like the warrior he is."

Takeo nodded, and with Takeo at the head and Mamoru at the feet, they carefully took him to the coffin. It was plain but functional, like Ryu would've wanted. They gently set him down before Mamoru pulled the sword from where it rested and laid it on the body. He fixed Ryu's hands so they grasped the sword on his chest before he stood up and took a step back. "Does anyone want to say anything?"

Takeo was the first to step forward, where he fell to one knee next to the coffin with his head bowed. "Ryu, my friend and brother. We had so many good times in life, and I'm sure when my day comes, we'll both chill in the hereafter, fighting and arguing over stupid shit...like we did in this life." He looked up, fire in his eyes as he crossed his arm over his chest. "I swear I'll find the one who did this. I don't care how long it takes, I don't care how far I have to look. I'll spend every waking moment looking for your killer, and I swear I'll avenge you." He stood up before taking a step back.

Makoto was the next to step forward. "Ryu, I have no idea what you thought of me. I think you thought of me like a little brother...you never saw me as I hoped you would. But that's okay, you were everything I needed; a confidant, a friend, a sword, and a shield. Thank you for everything you ever did...I'll never forget you."

He backed away and Mamoru walked forward, staring down at the serene face for a long time before he could bring himself to speak. "Ryu, I never told you this and I wish I had. But you were more than a student to me. You were my son, not by blood, but in every other sense of the word. If I could, I would switch places with you in half a second. I'm sorry I wasn't there to protect you. I never should've let you walk out that door, and I pray you can hear me now when I say, I'm so sorry...forgive me for my foolishness. I would do anything, pay any price, if I could change what happened today."

He bowed and closed the lid, then looked at Makoto,

who nodded. A breeze lifted the coffin before gently lowering it into the hole. Mamoru looked at the sky. "May the Kami watch and guide his spirit to the afterlife." He raised his hands and the slab of dirt moved, shifting before it tipped over and began filling the hole to the top. Takeo carried over a slab of wood that he had cut from a tree, and slammed it into the ground at the head of the grave. He had burned words into the wood.

Here lies Ryu Oda,
Friend brother and son.
Last of the Pure line.
May he rest in peace.

Mamoru nodded at the headstone. "It's fitting."

Takeo shrugged as he headed for the house, with Makoto following close behind. Mamoru was the last to leave, but only after he had bowed before the gravestone again.

"Forgive me Ryu." Mamoru slowly walked away with his head hung low.

***

Six feet underground, Ryu's body flashed and then was gone.

***

Ryu slowly opened his eyes and saw red clouds. He sat up and looked down at his body. There was no blood, no bones, and he was dressed in a jet black leather shirt that reminded him of his brothers…except his had tiny little pockets. He was also wearing a pair of black cotton pants and plain tabi shoes. He reached up to rub his eyes and found that there was a cowl on his face, but farther up his hair was free and waved back and forth as Ryu shook his head. He was dead, right? Then why was he in the Elder dimension?

He stood up and brushed himself off, and while doing

114

this, his right hand brushed against something. He grasped the blade by its hilt and pulled it up to eye level, and one word clicked in his head. "Kusanagi?" He nodded as he strapped the sword on his back, where, as his sword was in reach of his right hand, Kusanagi would be in reach of his off hand.

Who knows how I got it? I'll have to ask Mamoru when I get home. He looked around and found cracked earth in every direction, and growled.

"Damn it, how in the hell did I get here? I need to leave soon." He remembered what Mamoru had told him after his first trip here.

For every day that passes earth side, two years will pass here.

He knew he should be dead; he could still feel the blood pooling around him as his world had faded. "I need to get back before that bastard kills Takeo or Makoto." He gave one last glare at the sky before he started running to his right, figuring when in doubt, right is always right.

Chapter Eight:
Secrets and Truths

Three days had passed since they had buried Ryu…three days since Mamoru had slept, three days since Makoto had eaten, and three days since Takeo had said a single word. The home that had been so full of life was now shrouded in darkness; the sadness was so thick it hung like a dark cloud over all three, and no one spoke or made any excess noise besides what was absolutely necessary. Every day Mamoru would go outside and talk to the grave marker. Every day Takeo would sneak out his window and scour the forest for any sign of Ryu's killer, and every day Makoto would burst out crying at least twice a day.

The routine was broken when Mamoru felt a presence behind him. He whirled around, half expecting a man holding a sword, but what he saw froze him in his tracks. "Z-Zenaku!"

The white haired man gave a flourished bow. "Hello Sensei, did you miss me?"

Mamoru was shocked as Zenaku walked past him and laid a single white flower on the grave.

"We should always pay tribute to those who give their lives to make us stronger, right Sensei?"

He shot an insane grin at Mamoru as the situation donned on him. "You killed him?"

Zenaku shrugged as he turned towards Mamoru in time to block his sword. "I may have hastened his...fall."

Mamoru was seething with anger, both at Zenaku and at himself...this was all his fault. If he had killed Zenaku when he was supposed to, none of this would've happened. "Why? Why did you kill him?"

Zenaku blocked a series of attacks as Mamoru's sword flashed again and again, trying to slip through his defense. "I really didn't want to, but the little bastard left me no choice. You chose those three over your own son, and I have to admit that angered me a little."

Mamoru threw him back and Zenaku flipped and landed on Mamoru's house. "You think the Elders little shield could keep me from finding my ancestor? I say ancestor because I was alone in the Elder dimension for seven thousand three hundred years. I remember each day, trying to find my way home."

Mamoru felt his heart clench at these words as Zenaku shook his head. "I thought it was some kind of tough training. I spent all those years waiting for you to come back and say my training was over, that I could finally come home. But no...instead, I had to crawl through dimension after dimension until I finally found my own way home. I expected some kind of welcome home, despite our differences. Instead, I found those brats running around. Three kids had taken my place, and you never even mentioned me." Zenaku's grin turned malicious. "Finally I decided to take my place back...I would just kill them. So I lured the one who had taken my place into the forest and I killed him."

He threw back his head and laughed as Mamoru seethed with anger. He was about to launch himself at Zenaku when a yell stopped him. They both turned toward the sound as Takeo came flying out of the forest, his body engulfed in fire and his sword double edged, with fire licking up and down the blade. Takeo rammed into Zenaku and carried him into the air, where they proceeded to engage in a fierce exchange of attacks.

"You bastard, you killed Ryu!" Takeo attacked again and again, sending them higher and higher as Mamoru watched in apprehension on the ground, unable to reach them at the height that they had climbed to in mere seconds.

"Takeo, don't fight him; you're not strong enough."

Just then Makoto came running out of the house. "Sensei, I heard shouting. Is everything okay?" Makoto followed his sensei's line of sight to the two aerial combatants, before he took off into the sky with his sword drawn, and Mamoru shouting at them to stop. But on the ground he was powerless to stop them.

Zenaku laughed as he battled them both. It was effortless for him to block and attack, and they started to lose momentum. Zenaku flipped in the air and delivered a vicious ax handle kick to Makoto's left shoulder. There was a cracking sound before Makoto plummeted toward the ground, where Mamoru barely caught him before he hit the ground.

Mamoru looked back up just as Zenaku slammed the hilt of his sword into Takeo's face before he grabbed him by the throat and threw him towards the ground. As Takeo fell his wings flapped desperately, and as his free hand clutched his face blood leaked between his fingers. Mamoru caught him and Zenaku landed on the roof with a sick grin.

"This is the best they have to offer? Father, you have seriously been lacking in their training. I thought I got lucky with the demonic one and maybe he just couldn't think straight because of the pain, but now I know he wasn't a challenge because that was just the way he was trained." Zenaku chuckled as he sheathed his sword. Mamoru regarded him warily.

Zenaku shook his head, the same sick grin never falling. "Don't worry, I don't want to kill them yet. I want to wait before I take another one of your students from you. I'll wait until the pain will be at its highest peak, then I'll take that one." He pointed at Makoto as he sat up, cradling his arm.

"Then I'll wait and take that one." He pointed at Takeo as he pulled his bloody hand away from his face to reveal the blood running from his nose as he tried to staunch the flow.

Mamoru rose to his feet and drew his sword. "What makes you think I'll let you leave here alive?"

Zenaku chuckled as he held up his index and middle fingers. "One, you couldn't kill me then, and I doubt you can do it now, when I have over seven thousand years of experience on you, Father. And two...."

His index finger fell and Zenaku shook his head with a grin. "I'm not giving you a choice." As the words left his mouth a portal opened and he stepped through. Mamoru ran towards the portal but it closed before he could pass through.

"Damn it!" Mamoru rammed his sword into its sheath as he went to Takeo. "Are you alright Takeo?"

Takeo nodded before gesturing at Makoto. "Go make sure he's all right...I'm fine."

Mamoru went to Makoto and kneeled next to him as he cradled his arm. "Are you alright?"

Makoto shook his head as he looked at the spot where Zenaku had vanished. "He killed Ryu, and we couldn't stop him." Makoto looked away with tears in his eyes as Mamoru gently embraced him.

"It's alright Makoto, I'll talk to the Elders. They'll help." He heard Takeo scoff and turned to look as Takeo rose to his feet. His wings had disappeared and he glared at Mamoru.

"Ryu wouldn't want that...he never trusted them."

Mamoru looked at Makoto and could tell by looking into his eyes that he felt the same way. Mamoru sighed as he placed one hand on Makoto's shoulder and the other on his upper arm.

"This will hurt a little." Makoto nodded and with one swift motion there was a cracking sound followed by a pop, and Makoto had to bite his lip to keep from screaming. Mamoru gave a sympathetic wince as he ripped a large strip from his clothing and used it to wrap Makoto's arm in a makeshift sling.

"Still, they are the only ones that can fix this, probably by relocating us." Mamoru stood up and unsheathed his sword before cutting a hole between the dimensions, then re-sheathing his blade all in one practiced motion. "Come on. I'm not letting either of you out of my sight."

Together they all walked through and appeared in the main hall, where Nobunaga, Ieyasu, and Hideyoshi were waiting for them. Nobunaga had a small grin on his face as he regarded the three.

"Mamoru, what a surprise." Mamoru and Makoto bowed but Takeo only glared. Mamoru straightened up before he spoke.

"My lords, my students and I were just attacked by Zenaku." Mamoru didn't see any signs of surprise, and a small shred of doubt formed in his mind over whether Zenaku had found his own way to them or if he'd had some help.

"Yes, we had heard; also, we offer our condolences for the loss of Ryu. So very sad to hear that." His tone of voice made it very clear that he really didn't care, and Mamoru felt that shred getting bigger.

"My lords, my students and I need protection. Will you do nothing?"

Nobunaga seemed to consider it before he shook his head. "No, we will do nothing. I did warn you Hattori; you should've listened."

Mamoru placed his hand on the hilt of his sword. "If I find out that you had anything to do with Ryu's death, I will kill you."

Nobunaga chuckled as he held up his hand, and Mamoru fell to his knees holding one hand over his heart. "We do not take to threats kindly. Had we wanted Ryu dead,

121

we would've done it personally. Do not presume yourself a threat, Hattori; you don't have the power to back your claim."

He put his hand back on his throne and Mamoru started gasping for air.

"Now leave, and if you value what little of your life you have left, you will not come before the council again unless you are summoned." Nobunaga waved his hand and they were back in Mamoru's living room. Mamoru collected himself off the floor with a groan as Takeo and Makoto fussed over him.

"The Elders know something Sensei, I can feel it."

Mamoru looked at Makoto before nodding. "I'm sure they did, but for some reason they're not saying."

Takeo backed away and glared at the wall. "Goddamn bastards...Ryu was right. Whenever something goes wrong, the Elders are always at the heart of it."

Mamoru shook his head as he walked outside, Makoto and Takeo following closely. "Zenaku will not stop until you are both dead; we can't stay here any longer."

Takeo growled as he looked at his sensei. "Why is he coming after us?"

Mamoru sighed as he looked around, and his eyes locked on a tree where an unnatural shadow was lingering.

"Ten years ago, when I took you three in, the Elders forced me to abandon my student at the time; so I chose to leave him in the Elder dimension."

Makoto shook his head. "But, he called you Father."

Mamoru grimaced. "He was my student and my son." He walked away, leaving them to digest the information he had just given them. He walked into the tree line as the shadow followed him, and when they were deep enough in the woods Mitsuo appeared. He looked tired and ragged, but he didn't look how Mamoru thought he would.

"Mitsuo, let me explain; I—" He was cut off as Mitsuo spoke, his voice like gravel.

"Ryu is alive, Mamoru."

Mamoru felt his chest clench, wanting nothing more than for that to be real, but he knew he couldn't be. Mamoru had buried the body himself.

"Mitsuo, I'm so sorry for your loss."

Mitsuo spoke again, this time with more conviction. "Ryu is alive."

Mamoru shook his head, not willing to believe it. "Mitsuo, that can't be. I was there…you didn't see the body."

Mitsuo looked at him, his lightning blue eyes dancing with power. "I've seen him."

Mamoru looked at him. He had splotches of red dust on his clothing. "When? Where?"

Mitsuo leaned against a tree, using it to rest his body against. "Yesterday, in the Elder dimension. He's been there since the day you buried him."

Mamoru was in shock; on one hand he was deliriously happy, but on the other hand it couldn't be true.

"Mitsuo, it can't be...." A bolt of lightning struck despite the clear skies overhead.

"Think, Mamoru. Your other students are still alive…they still have their powers. How do you explain that?"

Mamoru was at a loss; Mitsuo was right. When Ryu died, Makoto and Takeo should've fallen into a downward spiral and they should be dead by now, but they were strong. Mamoru thought it was just the fact that the bond had never been allowed to mature. But Mitsuo was right, the moment life fled Ryu's body, the power should've gone back to Amaterasu until another host could be found. The gravity of the situation fell on Mamoru, and he found himself mimicking Mitsuo and leaning against a tree for support.

"Ryu's alive!" The words left his mouth before he could finish the thought.

Mamoru quickly thought about the time difference. Three days would be....

123

"Six years." Mitsuo spoke before Mamoru could finish his thoughts.

"He's been wandering the Elder dimension for six years, alone."

Mamoru felt his jaw clench before he took off towards the house. He ran through the door to find his students packing. "We're going back to the Elder dimension." Takeo didn't look up from his packing…he had withdrawn into himself again, and he barely heard a word his sensei had just said. Makoto was the one who spoke.

"Why, Mamoru-sensei?"

Mamoru didn't want to say anything until he saw Ryu with his own eyes.

"It's the safest place I could think of. Zenaku will think twice before attacking us in the Elders' own dimension." He unsheathed his sword and slashed the air; however, unlike every time before, no portal opened.

"What's wrong, Sensei?"

Mamoru looked at Makoto with shocked eyes. "I'm not sure; the only ones that can grant or suspend travel between the dimensions are the Elders."

Takeo snorted as he closed the bag holding his clothes. "They cut us off, probably to leave us to your son's insanity." And just like that he fell back into the tender shell holding him down. Mamoru shook his head as he too set about getting packed.

"We'll go to my old village. We'll be safe there; plus, they may have a portal we can use."

***

Half an hour later they stood in front of their house, their eyes not on the cottage but on the gravestone in front of it. Makoto looked at Mamoru with water-filled eyes.

"Do we really have to leave him behind?"

Mamoru nodded solemnly. "We can't bring him with us, we laid him to rest. It would be desecration to unearth him now." Also, he didn't want to have the opportunity to look in

124

the coffin...he was afraid of what might be inside. Together Makoto and Takeo lifted into the air and Mamoru dissolved into water. They all headed toward Mt. Fuji, where the Hattori clan kept their ancient village. As they flew Makoto tried to fill the empty air with conversation, but Takeo would have none of it and blatantly ignored him.

Takeo's eyes were focused forward, until Makoto spoke of the one thing none had spoken of since his death. "I wonder what Ryu would do."

Takeo faltered in his flight but quickly righted himself before he spoke. "I'm not sure what Ryu would do; he sure as hell wouldn't run, though, if it was one of us lying in that grave back there. He would rip this world apart; he would lift mountains to make sure no one was hiding under them. He wouldn't run, he'd sooner...." The sentence trailed off as the black shroud moved over them again. "He'd be fighting to make it right, is all I'm saying."

The conversation fell after that and the silence weighed heavily. Makoto didn't speak again for fear that Takeo would flip. He himself was half torn; he felt a darkness in himself that he couldn't place, but he felt he should know it.

"Its hatred." A voice spoke that he hadn't heard for days.

"Fujin?" He aimed the question inward and felt a soothing caress move over him.

"Yes Mako, who else could it be?" Makoto felt slightly comforted by the fact that he wasn't alone, because despite Takeo's pain, the only thing he'd accomplished with his silent treatment was to cause Makoto more suffering. He had no one to lean on; his only pillar had been knocked out from underneath him, and he was still falling. Takeo had fallen and had hit the bottom already, but Makoto was still in the throes of agony. Each day when he would awaken, Ryu's absence would hit him. He felt like his heart was being ripped out, and so far the pain was only getting worse.

"I miss him." He heard a soft cooing as he withdrew

into himself, his body naturally following Takeo as he shut down. He opened his eyes and found himself in a woman's embrace. She was beautiful, with long, flowing green hair that cascaded down her slender back. A small smile was on the lips of her kind face as she pulled Makoto closer to her. He welcomed the comforting feeling as he sobbed into her silver dress that flowed to her feet.

"Hush child, it will pass with time."

Makoto sobbed harder, and felt himself breaking when he heard Ryu's voice. "W*e don't have to be what the Kami intended, we can be whatever we want to be. If you want to let go and cry, then don't hide behind a barrier. Cry, shout. Scream. Whatever makes the pain stop!*" Makoto did just that; he'd screamed, shouted, and cried for three days, and he still felt the pain like a raw gaping wound. It felt like something was clawing his heart out.

"Easy child, you must rest. The pain will stop...this I promise."

He knew it would, it always did; but until it did, it caused unimaginable agony, like being cut with a thousand swords. Makoto withdrew back into his body and saw Mt. Fuji appear. He looked over at Takeo as he wiped tears from his eyes. Takeo was calm like a candle flame, and it surprised Makoto. He had expected Takeo to rant, rave, something! But instead, he acted like it didn't happen...or worse, like he didn't care.

***

Takeo focused on the task at hand, which was to keep his body moving forward, to not think about what Makoto had said. Ryu wasn't there, Takeo was...it was stupid to ponder what Ryu would do in their shoes...he couldn't do anything now, because he was...no! He wouldn't think it...if he did then it was real. It was bad enough that he had seen Ryu in that state—covered in blood when it should have been on the inside; cold, his bones scraping in a way that shouldn't be possible—that was both horrifying and sickening. He felt disturbed by the images, but he refused to forget them; to forget them would be like losing a part of Ryu, and he absolutely refused to let Ryu go. He was their leader, the glue that held them together, and with his passing that job fell to Takeo. A job he intended to take seriously, but even as he made the promise he felt he was betraying it. He couldn't feel anything, one of the points of being the Lord of Fire. Takeo couldn't feel multiple emotions, his mind could only process one at a time, while Ryu was the exact opposite.

Ryu had felt all the emotions like a bullet...they came one after the other and buried themselves deep inside him, where they began to fester and grow. Makoto, however, was the middle between them. He felt emotions through a controlled barrier, but when he felt, it was like a tsunami. Each had strengths and weaknesses, each helped the other by maintaining the balance.

With Ryu gone the triad was broken, and Takeo wasn't sure what he should feel. On one hand, he knew he should feel anger, but on the other, he knew he should feel sadness. Both emotions were warring for dominance, and he wasn't sure which he should feel, so instead he didn't feel anything. He just became a shell, a hollow vessel. Takeo was shaken from his thoughts as Makoto spoke.

"Takeo, do you seriously think we can pull this off without him?"

Takeo felt sadness steal the reins over his mind and tears filled his eyes, but he didn't turn in case Makoto would see. Instead, he looked ahead and responded.

"Of course Mako, I'm sure we'll manage."

Mt. Fuji was below them, and already Takeo could see signs of life. He dropped from the sky on the outskirts of a bustling town. He felt Makoto land next to him with half as much grace as he usually exuded.

"We should wait for Mamoru-sensei here." They sat across from each other and waited for their sensei, who couldn't be far behind.

***

Mamoru was the first to reach the mountain, and had used his power of water to slide up the mountain and reach his village a full thirty minutes before his students arrived. He looked around his ancestral home with a fond smile…every shop was a memory, every face a friend; but he didn't need friends.

He needed to find a dimensional rift that they could use to get to Elder, so he slipped behind buildings and around people. No one noticed him, and he found his way to the main house…his old home. He walked through the gates and up to the front door. The garden was just as he remembered, with a large koi pond and sakura trees dotting the yard. It was still as breathtaking as the first time he saw it.

The front door opened and a man who appeared to be late forties stood before Mamoru. He had short brown hair, a long scar across his face that started at his right cheek and extended across to the other, another scar placed diagonally down his left eye, plus dozens of other scars hidden from view by his clothing, but Mamoru knew each and every one of them from his long days of training with this man.

"Father, how are you?" He spoke with a deep bow; he had absolute respect for the man who was the patriarch of the Hattori clan.

"Mamoru, it's good of you to visit your old man after so many years." The man placed his hand on Mamoru's head before giving him a sound whack on the head. "And that's for not coming sooner."

Mamoru straightened up while rubbing his head with a sheepish grin. "I'm sorry Father, I had an engagement that I couldn't escape until just now."

His father made a sound in the back of his throat as he moved past Mamoru and into the garden. "You seemed perfectly capable of leaving your engagement to Kimiko before you were even married."

Mamoru sighed as he followed his father into the garden. "Father, you know that it never would've worked. Had I gotten married to her I would've had to leave her when the Elders commanded anyway. This way I left on my terms and there were no hard feelings. I mean, no hard feelings after she left a baby on my door step."

The older man snorted. "Calling the boy Zenaku was cruel of her; how is he these days?"

Mamoru looked away with a grimace. "He's dead to me."

His father turned around with a look of surprise in his eyes. "Such hatred. Tell me everything."

Mamoru proceeded to relay as much of his tale as he could until he was breathless from it. They had found their way to the porch and were sitting down by the time he was done.

"Well, that's quite a story, my son. I'm deeply sorry for your loss."

Mamoru shook his head as he looked over the garden. "Thank you Father, but no amount of condolences can make up for the loss of two sons."

The older man nodded as a messenger came running forward; he bowed before speaking. "Lord Hanzo, two men have been found on the outskirts of the village. What should we do with them?"

Hanzo turned to look at Mamoru, and the unspoken question was answered. "Bring them to me; do not harm them or detain them in any way."

The messenger bowed as Hanzo turned back to Mamoru. "So now I understand why you came here, but why to me?"

Mamoru leaned forward with an iron glint in his eyes. "I need to get to Elder, and my powers have been blocked."

Realization donned on Hanzo and he nodded. "First tell me why, before I grant you access."

Mamoru sighed as he leaned back. His father was a hard

ass at times, but he was a good man at heart. "I have reason to believe Ryu Oda is alive and wandering Elder. I need to go there and find him, no matter the cost."

Hanzo looked Mamoru over, and silence reigned as the main gate opened and his wayward students appeared. Mamoru didn't take his eyes off Hanzo, who in turn refused to look away as well. The gate closed as Hanzo nodded slowly. "Very well, my son, I will grant you access on the condition that you stay until nightfall. It will take that long to ready the gate."

Mamoru nodded his head. "Even though it causes me untold amounts of pain just thinking about how long he's been alone already, my students and I will wait."

Hanzo sighed slowly before he nodded. "Very well, you will be ready to leave by nightfall."

Mamoru stood up before he bowed. "From the bottom of my soul, thank you Father."

Hanzo waved off the words with a soft smile. "No thanks are necessary. Now introduce me to the runts that have stolen my son for so long." Mamoru smiled. Maybe, just maybe, it would be all right.

Chapter Nine:

Shackles

It was nearing nightfall, and as the sun went down Mamoru found himself wandering around his old home. The citizens had long since retired, and now ninja prowled the roof tops, silent, hidden defenders, each sworn to defend the village against any attack. Mamoru shook his head; a long time ago he was one of those ninja. Only he didn't do it for the safety of the village…he did it for the glory…the right to say he laid his life on the line for his village.

Mamoru chuckled as he turned down a side street to begin heading home. Shortly they would go through the portal, and before long he would have his three sons back. He felt the hairs on the back of his neck stand on end, so he turned around and found one of the ninja standing five feet away.

"Is something wrong?" Mamoru cocked his head but the ninja refused to speak. Instead, he pulled his cowl off and let it drop to the ground. Mamoru instantly tensed.

"Zenaku!"

The white haired man smirked as he looked around, then pulled a wicker hat from around his neck and put it on his head.

"Did you honestly think that you could hide here of all places? Come, Father, you're not even trying to make this

131

fun."

Mamoru drew his sword and Zenaku responded in kind. "What do you want?"

Zenaku chuckled and disappeared. Mamoru looked left then right, but Zenaku was nowhere to be found. Then he felt a point in the small of his back and a voice whispered in his ear.

"I've had a change of heart; rather than let you die, I've decided to kill you myself." Mamoru had barely enough time to take a step forward before he felt Zenaku's blade slide through him like he was butter. He stared down at the blade in disbelief. There was a clatter at the end of the alley and Mamoru heard someone shout his name before he fell.

***

Takeo and Makoto were getting ready to pass through the gate. Mamoru had ordered that if he wasn't back before the portal was ready, they were to go through without him.

"Mamoru should be here."

Takeo nodded as he looked at Makoto, who was wringing his hands. "He should be here, Takeo; why aren't you worried?"

Takeo gave a sad smile. "Maybe you're right; I'll go look for him." Takeo opened the door and was met by one of the Elders' royal messengers, who was flanked by three guards all wearing the same red samurai armor favored by the temple guardians.

"The Elders wish to see you, Takeo Toyotomi and Makoto Tokugawa." Without another word the guards walked in and seized them by their arms, but they made a single mistake; they had two guards hold Makoto and only one grabbed Takeo. Takeo broke the hold with ease, and with a lightning fast slash, split the guard down the middle. Takeo grinned viciously.

"That one is a Ryu original." He flew across the room and slew another guard before he could even draw his blade. The final guard had managed to draw his blade, but with a flick of his wrist, Makoto lifted him into the air and then proceeded to slam the defenseless guard into the floor repeatedly. "Die bastard, die!"

Makoto threw the guard through the roof with a shout, and found himself panting as he turned toward Takeo, who had a shocked look on his face. "Makoto, are you all right?"

Slowly Makoto reined in his control before he realized what he'd done; then he felt sick. He looked at Takeo with tear-filled eyes.

"Takeo, what's wrong with me?"

Takeo snorted as the portal opened. "There's nothing wrong with you Mako, you just got angry; it's all right. It's human."

Takeo looked at the portal just as six more guards came through. He readied his sword, but a sharp whistle stopped him cold. He turned toward the sound and found a man standing behind an unconscious Makoto. He was tall with short lavender hair and amber eyes, and wore a completely white outfit. And he had a blade to Makoto's throat.

"Enough fighting; come quietly...or, would you prefer this one to lose his head?"

Takeo didn't hesitate to drop his sword, and the man smiled. "Excellent." They walked through the portal, but instead of the world above they found themselves in a dimly lit dungeon. The man kicked a cell door open and threw Makoto in, and Takeo lunged in to stop him from falling as the cell door closed. The man stood beyond with a satisfied smile on his face.

"I am General Kohaku Fuma, and I'll see you at the execution tomorrow." Kohaku and his guards disappeared with their weapons, and Takeo threw himself at the bars.

"Let us out, you bastards!" His shouts reverberated off the walls but went unanswered. Takeo turned back to Makoto as he heard a sound. Makoto opened his eyes before shifting, and Takeo was at his side in a second.

"Are you alright?"

133

Makoto nodded as he sat up, rubbing the back of his neck.

"Yeah, he hit me and I passed out."

Takeo growled as he got up and threw himself at the bars again; they rattled, but gave no sign of moving.

"Don't bother."

Makoto and Takeo turned toward a calm and cold voice in the corner. Takeo quietly approached it.

"Who are you?"

He heard a sinister chuckle. "I don't feel the need to introduce myself, nor should you. Just stay on your side and I'll stay on mine." Takeo had gotten close enough to see a pair of smoky blue eyes staring at him from the darkness. The cell was so dim he doubted the stranger could see them any better.

"Hmm, suit yourself." Takeo went back to Makoto and sat down next to him. Makoto looked over but Takeo couldn't discern his expression.

"What did he mean by 'execution'?"

Takeo could hear the fear and sighed. "I don't know, we've done nothing wrong." He heard a snort from the corner and glared.

"And what did you do to get here. Huh?"

Takeo heard some movement and saw a shadow move along the wall before settling closer to the bars.

"I will be beheaded for the one murder I didn't commit."

Takeo didn't doubt this man was a murderer, he could smell the blood in the air. "What murder was that?"

The eyes turned toward him with a cold, calculating look. "They say I killed my sensei; that was a year ago."

Takeo heard Makoto get up and slowly approach the man. "You've been here for a year, in this darkness. By yourself?"

There was another sinister chuckle. "No, I've had cell mates…they just don't last long."

The outer door opened and Kohaku stepped through.

"Nobunaga wants to speak with you." Kohaku walked toward the cell and opened the door. The stranger stood up and walked toward the door.

"I'm going to kill you Kohaku, you realize that don't you?"

Kohaku chuckled as he slapped a pair of manacles on the stranger's wrists. "This time tomorrow you'll be dead Tatsu; how do you plan to kill me? From the grave?"

Tatsu replied by disappearing and reappearing behind Kohaku, with the manacles wrapped around his neck. "Just like this, only quicker."

Kohaku grabbed the chain and pulled it away from his neck. "You know as long as you wear these, you can't harm me."

Tatsu grinned as he walked into the outer area, which was slightly better lit. Takeo looked at his face; he was young...older than they were, but still young. His features were chiseled, he had a scar running down his right eye that stopped at the cheek, and as far as Takeo could tell he was wearing dark red clothing. A wicker hat obscured his hair.

"The shackles come off eventually...they always do; and when they do, I'll twist your head around so you can look me in the eye as you die."

Kohaku shook his head before he backhanded Tatsu toward the door.

"Maybe someday mongrel, but not today." They left the dungeon and Takeo and Makoto were alone again.

"Hmm, someone who hates that guy more than me; maybe Tatsu isn't so bad after all."

Takeo chuckled as the door opened again. This time a guard came in with someone following close behind. The guard bowed out and left them with the man.

"Hello boys." Takeo looked at the speaker with a glare, and finally recognized him in the darkness.

"Lord Hanzo Hattori. Where's our sensei?"

He heard Hanzo shift before speaking.

"Mamoru was killed before you were brought here."

The news hit them like a ton of bricks.

"That's not possible; we talked to him just an hour ago."

Hanzo shook his head as he sat down. "I'm sorry boys. I watched him die; he was killed by a man wearing a wicker hat."

Takeo immediately thought of Tatsu but dismissed it, because he had been there for a year, and as far as he knew, their sensei only had four students. Makoto started tearing up as Takeo grimaced. He didn't have any love for his sensei, but he still respected him, and his death only brought Ryu's back in full.

"That's horrible; but why are we going to be executed? We didn't do anything!"

Hanzo sighed as the door opened to signify his time was up.

"I'm not sure boys, but I'll find out what I can. If it's in my power I'll get you out of here, I promise." He left them to the darkness and the misery.

Ryu was dead and now Mamoru. People they knew were dropping like flies; before too long one of them would follow. Takeo looked around…there was only one door and no windows; no means of escape.

Light caught his eyes and he looked at the door. Red sunlight reflected under the door, signifying that morning had arrived. They didn't know when they had arrived, but by the looks of it Hanzo didn't have a lot of time to get them out.

The door opened and Tatsu walked in, followed by Kohaku. He opened the cell door and threw Tatsu in after taking the manacles off at knifepoint. Kohaku backed away with a grin.

"I'll send someone to collect you three in a few minutes." Then he was gone, and Tatsu sat by the door with a graceless slump. Silence reined until Tatsu spoke.

"When they come for us, I'm going to move fast; you

two can either keep up or you can die. It's your choice." Neither had any time to speak before the door opened and nine guards walked in. Tatsu stood up, backing away from the door. One of the guards opened the cell and the other eight walked in; four went to secure Takeo and Makoto, and four went to secure Tatsu. After a light struggle Takeo and Makoto were forced out of the cell, but Tatsu refused to move.

He was backed into a corner and had his eyes closed. The guard that had opened the door walked in and approached Tatsu. Suddenly his eyes snapped open and he was gone, appearing outside the cell and slamming the door shut. He locked it with a key he'd pulled from the guard on the way out; he snapped the key in half and threw it at one of the guards holding Takeo.

The key shot through his helmet and embedded in the wall next to the door. Takeo set to work by flipping on top of the other guard and snapping his neck. By the time he hit the ground, Tatsu had the remaining guards in the air, held aloft by their throats. With a single motion, he snapped both of their necks and dropped them to the ground. He walked to the door as the guards inside the cell tried breaking the lock.

"Move fast. You fall behind, you get left behind." He slammed through the door and was off and running, with Makoto and Takeo close behind. As they passed through the guards' station they saw their swords lying on a desk. They grabbed them as they ran past, and Tatsu was fastening two swords on his back as he led them down sunlit black hallways until they slammed into a dead end. They could hear sounds of armored feet approaching, and Takeo looked around before looking back the way they'd come.

"Now what, genius?" He heard a thoughtful sound from Tatsu and turned back toward the man who had engineered their escape. His earlier observation was right, except the dark red clothing looked more like old blood than coloring, and his right arm was bandaged from the hand to the shoulder. Takeo looked him over as he bent his legs with a single palm toward the ground, and without a word a ball of lightning formed in his hand before crawling up his arm. He slammed his fist into the wall with a grunt, then released a breath as a shout escaped his lips.

"ERUPT!" The lightning pulsed from his arm and ripped a large hole in the wall; sunlight bathed the hall in a red glow as Tatsu jumped through the hole down a nearly three hundred foot fall. Makoto was the next to jump, and Takeo growled as he followed closely. As they fell Makoto and Takeo sprouted wings and dived toward the ground, while Tatsu somersaulted at incredible speeds. He slammed into the ground and a crater formed in his wake; he simply straightened up before breaking into a run, while Makoto and Takeo followed from the air. There was nowhere to hide, not a tree within a hundred miles, but Tatsu drew a green sword from his left shoulder and slashed at the air.

Fifty feet out a dimensional rift appeared and Tatsu ran through it; seeing no other alternative, Takeo and Makoto followed. The darkness consumed them before they barreled into a forest, and they landed on the ground and found Tatsu bent over, sweating.

"Sensei was right; making one of those things with an exact location in mind is draining." He straightened before turning toward them with a grin; as soon as he laid eyes on them, the grin faded until all that was left was shock.

"Makoto, Takeo." The two backed away; they hadn't given him their names, and yet he knew them by a single look. Tatsu walked toward them and was met with the point of Takeo's sword. He didn't seem fazed as he looked at them, and the shocked look slowly turned into an anger filled smirk.

"I'm hurt; after seven years, that's how you greet me."

Their faces wavered and Tatsu pulled his wicker hat off. Makoto walked forward with a look of disbelief.

"It can't be...Ryu?"

Chapter Ten:
Reunion

Makoto couldn't tear his eyes away from their "fallen" teammate; he looked so alive, so mature, and so...furious!

"Well, nice of you two to finally show the fuck up. It's only been, what? Seven years? Yeah, I'm sure you've been busy!"

Makoto shivered; under Ryu's intense glare, his eyes danced with lightning. The air became heavy with the smell of ozone. The earth started quaking around them, and Makoto felt a flash of fear at the power that Ryu was holding back. "W-what? Ryu, what are you talking about?"

Ryu scowled at him as his hands flexed. "Of course, you both have no idea what I'm talking about. Why would you? You've never been alone by yourself with only the howls of demons as company. Neither one of you knows what it means to question the meaning of life. Neither of you has ever spent the day wondering if it's really worth it. With your only shred of hope dying a little more, until the only reason you can find for living is to see if you can; not because you want to, but because you need to know you're better than everyone else." He sighed and everything stopped; the ground stopped moving, the air returned to normal, and Makoto felt the fear finally leave.

"I know the very definition of hell. I've seen it, breathed

it, and lived it. You're both still children, still weak."

Makoto barely had time to process his words before Takeo flew towards Ryu and lifted him into the sky by the front of his shirt.

"What the hell are you talking about?" Ryu gazed into Takeo's eyes with a bone chilling coldness, not an ounce of emotion. He was a living stone. "We mourned for three days! We didn't sleep for three days! We cried for three days!" Takeo shook Ryu back and forth. "How dare you say those things to us? We buried you. You're the one that died!"

Ryu lifted his arms and slipped out of his shirt, landing on the ground without a sound and grabbing his swords as they fell out of the sky. Makoto gasped at what he saw; dozens of scars littered Ryu's body, more than he had ever seen on a person. But there was one over his heart, like some wild animal had tried to claw it out.

Ryu stared up at Takeo while the flying ninja stared down at him in horror. Ryu held both of his swords parallel to the ground by their hilts.

"No, I didn't die; if I did you would've known. Some part of you must've known that…some part should've known that. But it didn't, and do you know why?" He looked at them both as Takeo came back down and threw his shirt at him. He seemed to phase for a second before he stood still again, his shirt and swords where they belonged.

"It's because you're weak; you let petty emotions get in the way, and because of that you couldn't see the big picture, which is this: If I was truly dead, truly gone from this world, neither one of you could survive without me. You both would've perished within hours of my death. But you didn't, so the logical conclusion is, I did not die." He chuckled and they both felt a chill run up their spines.

Silence reined as Takeo and Makoto absorbed this; neither knew what to say. Neither wanted to say anything, because the fact remained Ryu was right. They had been taught since they were young to always protect one another.

If one fell, they all died.

"And that's undoubtedly why you both were sentenced to death...because I was sentenced to death."

Takeo shook his head as his right arm slashed diagonally in front of him, like he was pushing something away. "That's impossible; you wouldn't kill Mamoru."

Ryu cocked an eyebrow at him. "Wouldn't I? I had motive, opportunity, and more than enough time."

Takeo gritted his teeth. "No, you wouldn't. No matter what happened, you would never kill Mamoru."

Ryu shook his head with a solemn smile on his face. "Maybe I would, maybe I wouldn't. It's a moot point; the Elders think I committed an unauthorized murder, therefore I'm a felon and so are you. They know they won't get me again, therefore it's only logical that they will target you two. All they have to do is kill one of you and I'll die shortly after. Why go through a samurai's armor when the throat is so much easier to cut, right?"

He turned around and started walking before Takeo's voice stopped him. "Where are you going?"

Ryu looked over his shoulder, an unreadable expression on his face. "To find a man named Zenaku Hattori; he tried to kill me. I'm going to repay the favor." He pulled out his sword with the green hilt and slashed the air. Takeo ran at him just as the portal closed.

"Dammit!" Takeo looked back at Makoto to see him on the verge of tears.

"He really hates us."

Takeo scowled at the place where the portal had been. "No, he's just not happy with us right now. I'm sure he'll forgive us sooner or later. The question we have to ask is: How do we clear all of our names?"

Makoto nodded as he blinked the tears away. "We could go to the place where Mamoru-sensei fell and see if we can find any clues."

Takeo grinned. Things hadn't worked out as well as they

could've, but Ryu was alive; so long as that remained a fact, they had a chance to patch things up. "Right; do we know where it happened?"

"No, but we know he was walking around his village when it happened, so we should try there."

Takeo unfurled his wings with a nod. "Mt. Fuji here we come...again."

They took off into the sky, and only when they cleared the trees did they realize they had no idea where Ryu's portal had taken them.

***

Ryu stepped out into a quiet street. The moon was high in the sky, the walls were older, and the world around him was quiet. "*Ah! Hattori village, just like I remember.*" He put his wicker hat on and started walking. His first destination was the main estate, where he would be one step closer to finding Zenaku.

He must've been the one to do Mamoru in; it's better this way. Three birds with one stone; I'll get my revenge, I'll get justice, and I'll clear my name. He jumped over the main gates with a simple leap. Things had become easier over the last seven years. He had honed his powers faster in the seven years he had been alone than he had in the eighteen with his teammates. He snorted at the thought.

They called themselves his friends, his allies. But he hadn't seen hide nor hair of them. After he had found out Kusanagi's ability to transcend the dimensional planes three years ago, he had returned home only to find it abandoned. A slab of wood with his name on it had been all that was left. Not knowing where they could've gone, he simply went back to Elder. He didn't see any need to remain with echoes of the past, so he left, severing all ties to the past. *And now I find them and they act like I should just forgive and forget the seven years of loneliness without so much as an apology. Bastards! Both of them!* He heard a chuckle, one he had grown accustomed to during his long stay in Elder.

Why should they apologize? You're the one that died!
Ryu shook his head; he didn't have time to deal with Tenma,
the demon in his soul, one of the few things he'd had to talk
to. His only other sources of conversation had been Raiden
and the snake soul of the Kusanagi, which refused to be
addressed by any name but Orochi. It was annoying, but
they were the closest things he had to company, so he'd put
up with them.

Ryu knocked and a small boy opened the door. "Can I
help you, sir?" Ryu let his body relax and brought himself
down to the boy's level as he quirked a smile.

"Greetings. I'm looking for Lord Hanzo Hattori. Is he
present?" The boy nodded and closed the door. Ryu stood up
and walked off. He wouldn't get a warm reception, he knew
it. And really, why should he? He *was* a wanted criminal.

He gazed at the sakura trees with what little joy he
could muster. Before, these would have brought him
enormous amounts of joy just by standing under them. By
simply breathing in their fragrance he would've felt at peace.
Now he felt only disdain over all his wasted time under these
trees.

"So, you've returned. Was my son not enough, now you
must claim my life as well?"

Ryu looked over his shoulder and saw a middle aged
man standing by the door, his sword still sheathed in his left
hand and his right on the hilt. Ryu turned around before he
took a step back, then he gave a deep bow. "A thousand
condolences for your loss, Lord Hanzo, but I'm not the man
you're looking for."

The middle-aged man didn't look convinced, and Ryu
saw him starting to draw his blade. "My Lord Hanzo, I'm not
the man who killed your son. My name is Ryu Oda, and for
the last seven years I've been in Elder, which would be three
and a half days here." Hanzo's hand stopped as he looked
Ryu up and down with a slow steady look.

Ryu removed his wicker hat and Hanzo immediately

relaxed. "You're not the man who killed my son; the murderer's hair was white."

Ryu scoffed as he looked up some kind of divine joke.

"My son's murder amuses you?"

Ryu looked back at Hanzo and bowed his head. "I meant no offense, m'lord. The man who killed your son—my sensei—is also the man who tried to kill me. I was merely amused by the divine happenstance that would allow me to avenge both transgressions."

Hanzo looked confused but Ryu didn't offer up any explanation. "Is there anything else you can tell me about what happened after the murder?"

Hanzo shook his head. "I'm afraid not; he disappeared into a dimensional rift right after."

Ryu scowled. *If he went through a rift, there are any number of places he could be.* Ryu bowed again before he started walking toward the gate, and was just about to leave when Hanzo spoke.

"Who was it that murdered my only child?" Ryu stopped and stared at the ground. On one hand the man was very forthcoming; on the other hand he owed him no favors. After a long while Ryu spoke. "His name is Zenaku Hattori." He heard an intake of breath, but chose to walk away.

***

Makoto and Takeo had arrived at the village, and after an hour of eavesdropping, they had found out where Mamoru had been killed. They landed silently next to a red stain on the street; neither spoke as they bowed their heads in respect.

After they said their goodbyes, they looked up and found Ryu leaning against the wall. Takeo snorted as he regarded Ryu's cold visage. "What are you doing here?"

Ryu smirked as he kicked off the wall and walked around the sizable stain. "More than likely the same thing as you." He chuckled at their confused looks before he elaborated.

"Zenaku, the same man who killed me, also killed Mamoru."

Makoto gasped as Takeo growled. "That doesn't answer what you're doing here!"

Ryu cocked his head at Takeo. "Doesn't it? I want revenge and the man I'm looking for disappeared around here. I was hoping he had left a DRS, but too much time has passed."

Makoto shook his head as he slowly walked toward Ryu. "A DRS?"

Ryu glared and Makoto froze in place. "Yes, a dimensional rift scar. They happen when you open a portal without a dimensional arch, like the one located in the Hattori main home. If you don't use a dimensional arch you leave a scar in your wake. However, they fade within a day, depending on how large the cut is. Apparently the rift Zenaku cut was very small, because only hours have passed and his scar is gone."

Makoto shook himself from his stupor; so many things they had yet to understand and probably never would. "What do we do now?"

Ryu raised his eyebrow at Makoto. "*We*? I have no idea what *you* are going to do, but *I* am going to see someone who may help me locate that spineless piece of shit, then I'm gonna kill him." He turned around and pulled Kusanagi from its sheath, but before he could raise it he felt something latch onto his right arm. He whirled around, sword poised to strike, to find Makoto with his arm in a death grip.

"Release me!" He could feel the shift; he knew without having to look that his right arm had broken free of its wrapping, his eyes had bled to black, and he could feel his canine teeth had started to elongate. One look at Makoto and the fear in his eyes, and the speed with which he let go and jumped ten feet away, should've been enough to make him calm down, but it wasn't. "Don't ever touch me!" The threat was clear by his tone that bordered on hatred. He looked

145

down at his arm as the aura ate through his clothing; he closed his eyes and forced himself to calm. He slowly pushed his will into his arm, forcing back the possession. After almost a full minute, he opened his eyes to find that where his shirt had covered half of his arm, now it only covered three quarters of his chest. He turned toward the other two and opened his arms wide, Kusanagi still gripped in his left hand.

"See what I've become? This is why I hate you two; after I 'died' my right hand started to get steadily worse. Month by month it started to creep up my arm, and now it owns a quarter of my chest."

Takeo scoffed as he looked Ryu up and down; all signs of possession were gone...even Ryu's hand was normal again. "How is that our fault?"

Ryu shook his head with a slight smirk. "Not exactly yours; it's actually Makoto's. I just hate you by proxy; and before you ask, it's Makoto's fault because of the damn bond. I was away from him for so long that this infection spread faster than ever before. Now I have next to no chance to ever be rid of it." He turned away with a sardonic grin before he added. "Oh, and its killing me; isn't that wonderful? Before that happens I'd like to kill Zenaku. So you can understand why I don't have time to waste on you two." He raised his sword again before Takeo spoke.

"We can help you; we want that bastard dead too. If we all go after him, we have a better chance of killing him."

Ryu stopped. Takeo was right of course; three swords were better than one, and if worse came to worse he could always use them as a diversion. "Fine, but you will stay out of my way. The second you become more hassle than you're worth, I'll leave you in a dimension full of soul ravaging demons." He looked over his shoulder to see if his point had struck home and knew it had. "Alright, stay close." He slashed his sword downward and walked through the rift. He held it open as the other two walked through. Unlike their other travels through, there was no black tunnel. It was like walking through a doorway from one room to the next.

"That was weird."

Ryu shook his head at Takeo. "It's different when you travel from one place to another in the same dimension." He looked at Makoto and an almost nonexistent smile formed.

"Remember this place?" He turned to regard the Gothic-like castle in front of him as the sun rose behind them. Makoto spoke.

"Yes; this is Leonhardt's Castle, isn't it?"

Ryu nodded as he walked up the steps. Unlike last time he didn't smash through the doors, he merely knocked. The sound of his fist hitting the door reverberated loudly, and Makoto found himself flinching. Ryu dropped his hand and waited.

"What are we doing here?"

Ryu looked at Makoto before he turned back to the door. "I may not like Leonhardt, but he's always made it a habit to stay well informed, and usually he's like a walking Wikipedia. You input a search and he'll tell you what you want to know and then some."

The door opened and Makoto recognized Cassandra. She looked at Ryu with distrust, but brightened up the moment her eyes landed on Makoto.

"Dear Makoto! Oh, I'm so glad that you're here! Surely you can help!"

Makoto walked toward her and she embraced him like an old friend.

"Men from Elder came and took Lord Hellsing."

Makoto heard Ryu curse under his breath, saying exactly what Makoto was thinking. Ryu walked forward and bowed.

"Forgive my interruption, but I'm—"

Cassandra waved her hand. "I know you, Ryu Oda. Just because you've aged doesn't mean your blood has."

Ryu inclined his head as he rose from his bow. "Good,

that saves time, which is not on our side when the Samurai of Elder are involved. When was he taken?"

Cassandra backed away from the door as sunlight streamed in. "It couldn't have been more than an hour ago." Makoto turned from her to the sun and back again.

"Are the legends true about vampires and sunlight?"

Cassandra shook her head as she stared at Ryu, who had closed his eyes and seemed to be in deep thought. "Yes, but if you're old enough your body develops a tolerance to the sunlight."

Ryu opened his eyes with a definitive nod, as if agreeing to something he'd heard. "We have to leave now if we want any hope of catching up." He walked around for a second before he pulled out Kusanagi and slowly cut the air. "This would be the exact spot they vanished from, correct?" Cassandra nodded and Ryu put more of his weight into it as his sword started to get harder to push. Before long a rift appeared and he sheathed Kusanagi.

"It had almost healed, but it should still put us where they transported to. Let's just hope this doesn't end in a jail cell." He walked through and held the opening as Takeo walked through, followed by Makoto.

"Don't worry Cassandra, we'll rescue Leon."

Cassandra nodded as Ryu let go.

The portal slammed shut and they all walked toward the single point of light, but found that unlike before, it didn't get bigger as they got closer; if anything, it got smaller.

"Damn it, we'll have to force our way through."

Makoto heard Ryu's voice, which seemed to echo all around as something moved in front of the hole, blocking out the light; then slowly the hole got bigger. A large shape moved through the hole and Makoto heard a voice next to his ear.

"You're next."

Makoto dove through and found himself bathed in red sunlight. He looked at Takeo as he dusted himself off, then he looked back at the portal and found Ryu trying to force his way out.

Ryu had almost made it out when he lost his grip. "Shit!" His left arm was still inside the portal when it snapped tight around his arm like a rubber band. Ryu growled as it began to cut through the skin in an effort to close. Neither Makoto nor Takeo knew what to do, so they stood back.

Ryu's skin on his right arm started to crack and pulse, and his breath had started to come in short pants as he fought against the pain. He had no foothold to brace himself against. *"Don't panic Ryu. Concentrate!"*

Ryu could hear Raiden encouraging him and continued to pull, but the portal had started to cut into his skin and he knew pulling his arm out by himself would be almost impossible. Then he felt the skin on his back ripple and heard the tearing of cloth as large black, feathery wings spanned out, fourteen feet in each direction. They started to flap back and forth faster and faster. His feet left the ground and he started to hover as he beat his wings back and forth, harder and harder. All at once his arm ripped itself free of the rift's hold. He collapsed to the ground with his now skinless arm hanging beside him.

Makoto and Takeo watched in silent horror as Ryu pulled himself free; neither spoke as new skin started to form over the muscle. Finally his hand had fully recovered and Ryu looked at them with a grimace. "That is exactly why you never fight between dimensions. If there is someone on the inside, they can close it around you before you fully cross over." His wings folded and then disappeared as he looked around.

"Your wings are different."

Ryu's gaze settled on Makoto and he nodded. "Yours will change too, in a few years."

Ryu sighed. They were in Elder, and they were at the exact spot that Leonhardt's captors would have been, but he had no idea where to go next.

"This has been a waste of time and energy; we have next to no chance of finding him. Whoever took him has days if not weeks on us." He sat down with his legs crossed in front of him.

Makoto looked around before he shook his head. "So, what? We just go back and say that we searched for all of ten minutes before we gave up?"

Takeo looked between them, not sure who to go with. Part of him agreed with Ryu…they had too much of a head start, and without knowing which direction they went in, they could accidentally go the opposite way. On the other hand, he was still pissed at Ryu, so he didn't want to agree with him.

"I'm not saying that; I'm just saying this is very bad and we need a plan…so here's what we're going to do. I'm going to fly way up there and hope that they have had to make frequent stops between here and wherever they are going." With that he leapt into the air and quickly rose high enough that he could easily be mistaken for a bird if they were still on Earth.

Takeo sighed as Makoto sat down. "He's changed more than his looks and personality. He's not really Ryu anymore, is he?"

Makoto shook his head. "No he's not; he's the exact opposite of Ryu. He's cold, calculating, calm, and emotionless. It's like we got stuck with the mirror version of Ryu."

Takeo nodded, his eyes straying to the sky just as Ryu started to come back down. "Any luck?"

Ryu nodded as he pointed east of where they were. "I saw a band of samurai moving that way; some of them are hurt, so we should be able to catch up within half a day." Makoto got up off the ground as they all took to the sky and started heading east.

***

Ryu was right; within hours they all caught sight of the samurai and had to continue their pursuit on foot to avoid detection. Finally night fell; the sky went from spotted red clouds to dark ominous thunderclouds. Then the rain came. One second it was quiet, and the next they were bombarded with large chunks of hail. No one could hear themselves speak, let alone each other, so they relied on sign language, like their sensei had taught them.

Makoto asked, *"What the hell is this?"*

Ryu chuckled before he responded. *"It's natural...happens every night in Elder. You just better hope that we find shelter if we're stuck here too long, or you'll see exactly why the ground is barren."* Ryu exhaled and saw that both of them were shivering.

"Unlike you, they're not used to the harsh environment of this dimension." Ryu shook his head. Raiden was right, of course. Neither had experienced this kind of weather before, and the hail sure as hell wasn't massaging them right now. Ryu nodded as he waved for them to follow him. They jumped over the ridge that kept them from being detected and got within fifty feet of the camp before all at once, the hail stopped. Takeo looked up to see the hail bouncing soundlessly off a barrier of some kind.

"What is that?" Takeo kept his voice low.

Ryu responded in kind. "It's a barrier that the samurai erect; it will protect us from the hail, and in the morning it should be enough to hold back the sun."

Makoto could tell that meant something bad, but chose not to say anything as they hid behind some tents. Ryu looked around the tent before he returned to his place.

"There are twenty of them. They have Leonhardt shackled at the edge of the camp."

Makoto looked out from behind the tent and found that Ryu was right; Leonhardt was shackled to a cart that kept him chained down by his ankles, legs, waist, stomach, chest, wrists, elbows, neck, and head. Makoto retreated with an incredulous look on his face, and Ryu snorted.

"They are really underestimating him."

Makoto looked at Ryu and found not a trace of humor on his face. "What?"

Ryu shrugged as he closed his eyes in thought. "When they captured me, they had me shackled so tightly. Even my fingers were chained to the cart!" He opened his eyes and pulled out his sword. "All right, here's what we're going to do. I'll lead them off, while you two unchain Leonhardt; but wait until I get back to move him."

Makoto shook his head. "No, that can't work. You can't take on all twenty by yourself."

Ryu smirked as he cracked his neck. "I failed to mention that the reason why I was chained so thoroughly was that I killed one hundred of them before they managed to bring me down. By all accounts, this should be four times easier."

He ran out of hiding and managed to kill two of the guards before the rest even knew what happened. Ryu stood in the middle of them with a bloodthirsty smirk on his face. "Anyone else wanna cross swords with a demon?" He jumped out of the circle and dashed out of the protective bubble, with the samurai close on his heels.

Makoto and Takeo ran toward Leonhardt and started to undo his restraints as the vampires head lolled back and forth. "Man, he is really out of it," Takeo observed as he helped to undo the shackles.

Makoto nodded as he undid the final strap. Leon's body started sliding down the cart so they lifted him up, each supporting him by his arms, with Takeo under his left arm and Makoto under his right. Leonhardt's head rolled toward Makoto, who couldn't help but smile. He looked so peaceful, like he was merely resting.

Then he opened his eyes and Makoto's smile faded. His eyes were entirely red and his gaze was trained on Makoto's neck. Makoto barely had time to open his mouth before things went straight to hell.

Leonhardt threw Takeo away as his right hand flashed out and grabbed Makoto by his throat. Makoto watched as Takeo went flying, his body slamming into the ground with enough force that Makoto could hear something crack. Then red eyes blocked his vision out as Leonhardt forced his head to the side, trapping his arms with his free hand as Makoto tried reaching for his sword.

"Leon! What are you doing?" His question was answered as Leonhardt slowly descended on his neck. "Leon no. Don't, please don't!" His pleas went unheard as he felt the points of Leon's fangs on his jugular.

Chapter Eleven:

Bonds

Takeo looked up from the ground to see Leon leaning over Makoto. He tried to get to his feet, only to drop back down when his left leg refused to hold his weight. He watched in horror as he caught sight of Makoto's face; he had gone pale, and the fear in his eyes was enough to tell Takeo that Makoto had no way out. Just as Takeo had started to despair, something flashed across the camp, and the next thing he knew, Leonhardt was flying past him. Takeo looked back at Makoto to see Ryu slowly lowering him to the ground.

Takeo could see the side of Makoto's neck that Leon had been leaning over and saw no blood. Ryu disappeared and Takeo felt arms around him, and the world seemed to phase as he appeared next to Makoto, who seemed to have passed out. The shock of what almost happened combined with suddenly being whisked away at break neck speed was too much to keep straight in Takeo's mind. He was lowered to the ground and Ryu walked in front of him.

"I said to wait until I got back before trying to move him." His voice was low and cutting; those simple words said everything without needing to waste words. Ryu was angry, and frustrated that they had ignored him. "Stay here while I handle him."

Takeo forced himself into a sitting position. "What the hell's wrong with him?"

He heard Ryu chuckle as he stared down the irate vampire. "He's hungry."

***

Ryu looked at Leonhardt's red eyes, which were trained on Makoto, his canines elongated, his hands curved into claws. *You don't want my blood, you want his.* Ryu grinned; it would be easy to take him down if he didn't have to worry about his own neck. All he had to do was keep Leonhardt away from Makoto.

Simple in theory; let's see how it works in practice. Ryu watched Leonhardt; he was perfectly still...years of practice, years of experience he had killed to attain, because it was a simple fact...Leonhardt was a killing machine; but then again, so was Ryu.

They disappeared at the same moment, both meeting in mid air; neither let up...they both had the same drive, the same goal in mind: Survival. It was a basic instinct, something Ryu had come to rely on in the wastelands of Elder. They exchanged blows, both battling for dominance.

Unlike his battles in the past, this wasn't a battle of metal. It was a battle of the beasts; neither would give an inch, and when they separated they were still. Each had scuff marks on them, but neither had managed to draw first blood. Not because they couldn't, but simply because each had every reason not to.

Ryu knew better then to bleed Leonhardt; if the vamp started to bleed, Ryu wouldn't be able to get near him due to the risk of infection. While Leonhardt didn't want to bleed Ryu for the fact that the beast in him knew it would only serve to draw his attention away from his intended prey.

Leonhardt disappeared again, but this time Ryu didn't follow...he could see him. His body caused ripples as he dashed past. He was single minded. He had no fear...he was the perfect monster. Ryu let him go past before he followed, a mere step behind Leonhardt.

As Leon bent down, his fangs poised to strike Makoto's unprotected neck, Ryu lashed out with his left arm and wrapped it around Leonhardt's face. Ryu's wrist slid into Leon's open mouth and with a vicious pull, he felt Leon's fangs pierce his skin, and Leon felt a bountiful warm substance pour down his throat. It was only when the vampire opened his eyes that he realized he was being pulled away from his intended victim. He tried to pull his mouth off the pulsing vein, and in retaliation Ryu grabbed him by his hair and forced him to stay attached. More of the blood flowed down Leon's throat, and he finally surrendered to the offered vein.

Leonhardt latched onto Ryu's wrist with his hands and his teeth tore into the flesh like an animal, anything to make the blood flow faster, anything to make the hunger abate. Behind him, Ryu let go of Leon's hair, reasonably certain he wouldn't run. Ryu grimaced as he heard Leon groan with pleasure. *Damn animal.* Ryu looked over Leon's head to Takeo, who stared in horror, and Ryu snorted with amusement.

***

"Don't worry, I'm not gonna vamp out. His blood would have to get in an open wound or I would have to ingest it for that to happen." Takeo nodded as he looked away, finding the sight before him almost erotic, for it seemed oddly intimate. If Takeo didn't have such a firm grasp on his imagination, he could almost imagine Ryu enjoying it, his eyes half closed as he gently caressed Takeo's face...Takeo's head snapped back to Ryu and Leonhardt's position in shock.

Where the hell did that come from? He heard internal laughter and forced his mind inward, to an ancient Japanese Shinto temple. Pillars reached from the floor to the ceiling and each was adorned with a scroll just as long. Sitting in the center of the room before an altar was a man donned in red samurai armor that had seen better days. Clutched in his right hand was a red flaming sword. Takeo walked toward him, his injuries in the real world disregarded in the mind.

"Well, you going to explain what the hell that was?" Again the laughter; it was deep and booming, and echoed off the walls and reverberated around the room.

"It wasn't my doing little one, that was entirely of your own creation." The man stood up and faced Takeo, his face worn and scarred. If Takeo didn't know him, he would think this was one of the agents of the Elders. But he knew exactly who this was…it was Bishamonten, the God of War, the Japanese kami all warriors prayed to for protection and the strength to vanquish their foes.

"My making? That's impossible…I don't see Ryu like that. I-I like Makoto!"

Bishamonten chuckled as he nodded. "Yes. You sound sure of yourself; how could one doubt you with conviction like yours?"

Takeo growled, but then slowly memories started flowing back. Old ones. Times before he even knew about any sort of bond. How he had loved Makoto since they were kids. More memories came to the forefront of his mind, newer ones, fresher ones, and slowly, he started to realize his love had transformed…or maybe it had just shifted direction, and was more of a family love then anything deeper. "It doesn't matter. Just because I don't have feelings for Makoto anymore doesn't mean I have feelings for Ryu now. That's absolutely impossible!"

Bishamonten nodded as he sat back down. "Yes, but has anyone told you that you doth protest too much? Maybe these feelings are not unwarranted. He has saved you an almost inconceivable number of times. It's only natural that you would start developing something deeper for him. All I'm saying is, don't throw away a chance at happiness, just because you don't understand it." Takeo blinked and he was back in the camp. His leg had started to throb and Leon was still feeding on Ryu, both of them on their knees now.

***

Ryu grimaced. Leonhardt was insatiable. He just kept drinking, and Ryu's vision had started to blur. *I have to get him to stop; my blood can't regenerate as fast as my flesh.*

Ryu growled and tried to pull his arm back, but Leonhardt had a vice grip and wasn't going to stop until Ryu stopped bleeding. "Leonhardt, get the hell away from me." The vampire didn't move and Ryu was running out of options, so he did the only thing he could think of. His right arm cracked and started pulsing as his fingers narrowed into claws.

Ryu grabbed Leon by the back of his neck and ripped him off his wrist. Leon lunged forward and tried to get his teeth back into flesh, but Ryu's grip was solid. He stood up, taking Leon with him, and as Leon tried to latch onto him again, Ryu growled and slammed the vampire into the ground with enough force to dent the ground and crack a few of the vampire's ribs. "Leonhardt van Hellsing, snap the fuck out of it or I'll hold you here until the day you die." The vampire responded by growling and pushing against the ground.

"I said...." Ryu lifted him four feet off the ground before slamming him back down. "Snap out of it!"

All at once, Leon stopped moving. Ryu glared before he heard a voice. "Ryu?" Ryu let go and Leonhardt pushed himself to his feet as he looked around. He wiped some blood off his mouth before his eyes shot to Ryu's wrist. "What has transpired?"

***

It took awhile but Ryu explained everything he knew about what happened, including why he was older. At the end of his story Leon kneeled in front of him with an arm crossed over his chest. "I owe you a thousand apologies for *my* actions, and a thousand times over, you have my sincerest gratitude for *your* actions." Ryu waved his words away as he helped Takeo set his leg.

"I had little alternative, but if you want to show your thanks, you can tell me where I can find Zenaku." Leonhardt looked around, and looked at Ryu before he nodded.

"If we're where I think we are, then Zenaku Hattori makes his home two days north of here."

Ryu grinned before he caught sight of the sun on the horizon. "Leonhardt, the vamp chick we spoke to at your castle said if you're old enough, the sun has no hold on your kind. I hope for your sake that holds true."

Then the sun rose over the mountains and the world was bathed in fire. It was like a tidal wave, and battered against the shield. Fire rushed around them but it couldn't touch them. The temperature rose and rose, until all at once it was gone. The shield fell and the heat fell drastically until it became bearable.

"And that's why no one should walk this world without a shield; if the nights don't kill you, the mornings will."

Ryu wiped the sweat from his brow as someone groaned. He turned around and found Makoto starting to awaken. Ryu looked between him and Leonhardt with a small grin. *This ought to be fun.* He stepped back as Leon walked toward the recovering Makoto.

***

Makoto blinked away the blurriness as he slowly sat up, and felt someone at his left elbow urging him forward. "Uh, ouch. What happened?" He opened his eyes and was met with the color red circled by white. Images clicked, and he jumped away, drawing his sword as he went.

"Stay back!" He brandished his sword in front of him with a panicked look in his eyes. He quickly looked to the left as he heard a chuckle, and found Ryu standing with his arms crossed. "This is funny to you?"

Ryu shrugged as he walked toward them. "Yeah, a little. But, let's relax before things get out of hand."

Makoto shook his head violently as he kept his focus on

Leonhardt, who hadn't moved from his kneeling pose. "Out of hand? He tired to suck on my neck!"

Leon rose with his hands held up. "If I might interject. It is not entirely my fault…you have a very lovely neck."

Ryu chuckled as Makoto turned red. "I did tell you not to move him. I'd figured they didn't feed him and he would be lost to his lust."

Makoto glared as he sheathed his sword and stayed as far away from Leon as he could. "I'm still not happy with you."

Leon bowed to Makoto the same way he had to Ryu. "I'm sincerely sorry for what I did, and I hope one day you will be able to forgive me."

Ryu hung his head and sighed. "Listen, not that this doesn't touch a demon in his black heart, but there's someone out there right now waiting to die; so let's go." He heard someone clear their throat and found Takeo pointing at his leg.

"Busted, can't walk, can't fight; does any of this ring any bells?"

Ryu growled as he pulled out Kusanagi. "Fine, you've served your purpose anyways." With a flick of his wrist Ryu was gone, leaving behind three shocked people. Leonhardt was the first to recover.

"Well, he certainly hasn't lost any of his charm."

Takeo growled as his wings came out, lifting him into the air. "I can't fight, but I can fly. Let's find him so I can give that ass a piece of my mind."

Makoto turned to Leonhardt, who waved.

"Go. I'll follow on foot; I may not be as fast as you, but I will be close behind." Together Takeo and Makoto took off, heading north, hoping they wouldn't be too late.

***

Ryu looked down at barren landscape with distaste…there was nothing for miles around. Thinking wherever Zenaku was hiding might've been camouflaged, he dropped from the sky to resume the search on foot. *He's here somewhere.* He felt his pulse quicken at the thought of what was to come; he closed his eyes and could almost feel Zenaku's blood on his hands. The beautiful sounds of his voice, while he cried out in ecstasy as Takeo....*WHAT?* His eyes flew open as his thoughts caught up with him. His pulse had doubled in speed, his stomach felt like it was flipping.

What the fuck was that about? He would've passed it off as one of Tenma's tricks, but it was too far off his usual antics. After a few seconds to calm himself, he started running, hoping Zenaku would appear so he could be done with this place once and for all. Then he would...he stopped dead as the thought struck him. What was there after this? He had only planned so far as killing Zenaku. After that...he drew a blank. There was nothing...he couldn't go back with Takeo and Makoto. They no longer had a sensei, and they sure as hell couldn't trust the Elders with whoever they put in charge. He no longer had a purpose; there would be no more missions. Mamoru was gone. He tried to walk forward but his feet wouldn't move; he was glued to the spot as realization hit him like a ton of bricks.

I no longer have a reason to live. After Zenaku it would be over...no more missions, no more bickering, no more *anything!* His mind whirled with these thoughts as he sank to the ground. He retreated into his mind and found himself in the white room. Raiden was there, as was Orochi and Tenma, all arguing over some trivial matter; with a single thought the room flashed black before returning to its regular color, all eyes turned to him.

The snake Orochi was the first to speak. "What troublesss you, young one?" Ryu explained his problem and Tenma burst out laughing.

"That's what has your panties in a twist? Get over it! Kill Zenaku and then ask the oh so pivotal question: What now?" Ryu looked at Raiden, who inclined his head.

"Though not as elegant as he could put it, yes, I have to

agree with him. You've been pushing your limit for seven years for this day. While you may not know what comes next, you can only push forward and fight."

Ryu nodded and he was back in the real world. He got to his feet and started running. The landscape was flat except for a crater that could easily house four dragons. Ryu pulled out Kusanagi and slashed the air before sheathing his blade, then walked in and appeared by the crater. He looked over the edge and found a small hut at the bottom. *He must be here.* Ryu looked around and suddenly an idea struck him. He pulled out his sword.

"Come to me Raiden." Instead of curving into a half moon, only the tip curved now. The blade had changed when he had started to use two swords instead of one.

I'll bury him alive. Ryu's wings came out and he leaped into the air over the crater. He took a deep breath before he started slashing at the walls and ground. Each attack sent out a curved bolt of lightning, and within seconds, the walls crumbled and started filling in the hole, burying the hut and whoever was inside alive. Ryu stopped as soon as the avalanche started, and when the dust cleared, he dropped into the crater that was now bigger, but not nearly as deep.

"I wonder if that killed him?" Ryu had just closed his eyes when he heard someone speak.

"No, but it did ruin my home." Ryu whirled toward the voice to find Zenaku staring at him with a sneer on his face, wearing the exact same clothes Ryu had last seen him in.

"I don't know who you are, but I doubt I did anything that could warrant *that!*"

Ryu chuckled, glad he still had his sword in hand. "Oh, believe me, you deserved it. You also deserved to die under all this dirt, but I guess I can still do that once I'm done with you."

Zenaku unsheathed his sword and shook his head. "Wow! I must've done something really bad to upset you...do tell!"

Ryu disappeared and reappeared in front of Zenaku, and with one vicious punch to the face Ryu set him crashing into the wall of the crater. "My name is Ryu Oda, and I'm going to kill you!"

There were a few seconds of silence before Zenaku emerged, shaking his head in disbelief.

"No, that's not possible. I killed you years ago!"

Ryu grinned as he brandished his sword in front of him. "Oh yes. You did! But I crawled out of hell just for the sole purpose of killing you."

Zenaku growled as he flashed toward Ryu. They traded blows before one of Zenaku's attacks slipped through and cut a bloody slash through Ryu's already tattered clothing. Ryu placed his hand against the wound and as it healed, he glanced at the blood with a grin before he looked at Zenaku, who had a triumphant look in his eyes.

Ryu resumed his stance, his legs spread evenly apart and his sword held in front of him with both hands. "Not bad, but my question is: Can you do a thousand more just like it?"

Zenaku shrugged as he relaxed. "I'm not sure, but I have a question for you." Ryu remained silent and a wolf like grin spread over Zenaku's face. "How are you against poison?"

Ryu looked confused before he started swaying. Ryu's sight was blurred, and everything had an after image like he was drunk. "What the hell did you do to me?"

Zenaku grinned as he walked toward Ryu. "Oh, nothing. My blade's just coated in a very rare poison that comes from a snake in this wasteland."

Ryu's eyes widened even as he grinned on the inside. "The spirit of the eight headed snake demon Orochi?"

Zenaku clicked his tongue. "The one and only; it may be dead, but its venom is said to have the power to kill anything...even a god. That's why they put it here instead of letting it cross over."

Zenaku walked up to Ryu and grabbed him by the hair.

164

"The venom will burn you up from the inside out, then it will slowly begin devouring you until there is nothing left. It's quite horrific." Zenaku released Ryu and started walking away. Ryu lunged to his feet and rammed his blade through Zenaku's body. Zenaku turned, shock the only emotion on his face.

"How?"

Ryu smirked as he jumped away, then held up his bloodied sword with a grin. "You're not the only one with secrets. Like any poison, if you expose yourself to it you can become immune. And I had a little run in with Orochi awhile back, so I claimed some of its venom for myself and slowly started working on my immunity. Now it's only mildly disorienting, but it flushes itself from my system rather quickly."

Zenaku smirked as his wound sealed itself. "Very nice, little Ryu; I never would've guessed you had done something so drastic without your sensei."

Ryu closed his eyes for a split second before he glared at Zenaku. "Yes, my sensei is dead, and before the end of this day, you will join him."

He flickered before he was gone. Zenaku looked all around but there was no trace of Ryu anywhere. Just as he started to relax his stance, Ryu appeared and drove his knee into Zenaku's gut with enough force to lift Zenaku into the air. There Ryu brought the pummel of his sword and drove it into the back of Zenaku's neck, forcing him to the ground, where Ryu flashed out and kicked Zenaku away like he was trash. In the span of half a second Zenaku was thrown across the crater and to the opposite side.

Ryu watched as Zenaku slid twenty feet and came to a screeching halt as he rolled to his feet, a look of rage on his face. "You little bastard! How dare you? I'm superior to you. I killed you once! I'll do it again!"

Ryu made a sweeping arc with his sword and Zenaku had to dodge a lightning fast bolt of electricity. "You may

165

have been stronger than me then. Hell, you may be stronger now. But you lack the one thing that I have."

Ryu phased again and appeared behind Zenaku, wrapped his arms around him, and took off into the sky. Zenaku struggled as the ground got smaller and smaller, until Ryu finally let him go and the momentum carried him higher into the air before he started to fall. As he passed Ryu on the way down, Ryu spoke. "I have focus, a drive to be as powerful as I can be. You have no drive; you do whatever you want." Zenaku fell past him and Ryu flipped in the air and followed him down, locking his arms around him and carrying them, head first, toward the ground.

"No more Zenaku; my sensei may not have been able to erase your taint from this life, but I will. I'll pulverize you, and when you can't take it anymore, I'll send you screaming into the afterlife."

The ground was rushing toward them faster and faster, and Ryu started to feel the panic pouring off of Zenaku. "I'd tell you what it's like, but I'm sure I went to a different place then what you are bound for."

The panic got worse and Ryu could tell the panic wasn't entirely Zenaku's, it was coming from within. He closed his eyes and heard Raiden answer his silent question. "Makoto."

***

They had been flying west when it happened; a slab of earth the size of an elephant erupted from the ground and rammed into Takeo head on, throwing him to the ground with the slab lying on top of him. Makoto moved to go after him, but there was a flash of movement, and he barely had time to dodge before another slab of earth was thrown his way. He landed on the ground with Takeo lying within a hundred feet of him. Takeo struggled to get the earth off himself. Makoto looked ahead and saw the smirking faced of Kohaku Fuma standing across from him. "So, this is where my little jail birds went."

Makoto glared as he shifted his left foot back, about to

break into a run toward Takeo when a wall of earth erupted behind him. Kohaku lowered his hand and wagged his finger at Makoto. "Tsk tsk. You're gonna make me think you don't like me."

Kohaku disappeared and reappeared behind Makoto. "You don't want that, now do you?" Makoto felt a point of a knife at the base of his spine and froze.

Kohaku chuckled as he prodded Makoto forward and started leading him toward Takeo. "Now that is much better; let's go check on your friend before he gets the wrong idea."

They walked around the wall and Makoto's eyes locked on Takeo, who was fighting just to draw breath. His face was red and his teeth clenched with the effort of trying to push the earth off himself. He had just found a leverage point that allowed him a brief reprieve when the earth was pushed back down.

Takeo's eyes locked on Makoto as he came into view. His heart was pounding so loud that he couldn't hear anything, and the edges of his vision were starting to go red as Makoto was led in front of him. Takeo glared at Kohaku as his pinky lowered and the slab got even heavier.

Makoto was starting to panic. He couldn't move or Kohaku would stab him. But he couldn't just stand there while Takeo was dying from suffocation. "Stop! Please stop! You're killing him!"

Kohaku chuckled again as he applied even more pressure, and he could swear Takeo's eyes were about to pop out of his head. "Why should I? You two were supposed to be dead a full day ago. I should just crush him now and call my job done." Kohaku applied more pressure and Takeo's eyes rolled into his head as he fell limp.

Makoto felt the icy grip of panic clench around his heart as Takeo stopped breathing. He heard Kohaku whisper in his ear, "Just a little more and he'll be a red stain in the middle of this desert." Makoto knew he only had one chance, so he started to push away from Kohaku when they both heard a bestial roar. Makoto had expected Leonhardt to come from behind them and save the day, but instead he got Ryu, his eyes a soulless black, both of his arms overcome with dark, red spidery veins. He slammed into Kohaku and sent him flying away. Next he walked over to Takeo, and with one kick he sent the fragmented earth away from Takeo's prone body.

Ryu looked back at Makoto and growled, "Deal with him, I've got the other one." He looked at Kohaku, who had managed to get to his feet before Ryu went after him, and the air around him exploded as he ran.

Kohaku barely had enough time to blink before Ryu's fist slammed into his stomach and sent him into the sky; the ground cracked and exploded again as Ryu leapt after Kohaku. He appeared above Kohaku and flipped, delivering an ax kick that sent Kohaku spiraling toward the ground. He slammed into the ground, making a small crater. Ryu flew at him again when another body slammed into him.

Ryu flew away before correcting himself and glared at the newcomer, who flicked his white hair out of his eyes. "I wasn't done with you, beast." Zenaku grinned as Ryu flew at him, but was met with a sword that dragged itself across his chest. Ryu dashed away as Kohaku came to stand between them.

"This monster is mine." Kohaku fell into a battle stance with his sword held in front of himself; Ryu looked between them, quickly weighing his odds before he slowly unsheathed his sword and dashed after Kohaku.

Right as he was about to cleave Kohaku in half, Zenaku dropped down and forced him to dash away again. Zenaku stood up before sighing. "Let's team up for right now, since he doesn't seem to like either of us. Once he's dead we'll kill each other to see who's better." Kohaku looked Zenaku up and down before nodding.

"If you're so eager to die, fine."

Ryu growled as he dashed at Zenaku, but Kohaku

blocked his attack and he danced away right into Zenaku's blade. Within seconds, they had him backing away from their continued onslaught, and it was all Ryu could do to keep from being killed. His eyes followed them both; they worked like a well trained team, flipping over each other's attack and sliding their blades under, around, and behind, simultaneously blocking and attacking for each other. Each slash on Ryu's body barely healed before another was inflicted. Ryu jumped back out of the blades' reach and clutched a nasty wound on his right bicep. He growled as a red slit appeared in his eyes. "Admittedly you two are the toughest enemies I've ever encountered."

Zenaku chuckled as he lowered his sword. "Flattery will not earn you any mercy." Standing shoulder to shoulder with Kohaku, they were an impressive unit. Each knew what the other was gonna do before he even did it, and Ryu knew before long they would get the better of him.

Ryu could feel his strength failing him; his knees wobbled ever so slightly and his sword arm was starting to go numb. Each blow he delivered was met with the relentless strength of a mountain, and then returned with the ferocity of a dragon. "I mean only to pay my respect to the dead before I wipe you two mongrels from the face of existence." Ryu allowed a dark chuckle to erupt from his throat; his words were hollow and as weak as he was starting to feel.

Ryu felt the shadow of panic from earlier and his eyes moved to Makoto, who had succeeded in reviving Takeo, and together they followed the battle with rapt attention. Ryu grinned as an idea ran through his head; he poured some of his remaining power into the shriveled bond between them and sent a single thought to him. *"Makoto, rouse a sandstorm around us, now. Don't worry about me."* His eyes moved away and missed the way Takeo stiffened, and looked around for the disembodied voice that had just spoken to him.

169

***

Takeo averted his eyes as someone whispered in his ear; he looked at Makoto, expecting a reaction from him, but his eyes stayed glued to the battle in front of them. "Did you hear that?"

Makoto looked at him with confusion written all over his face. "Hear what?"

Takeo shook his head and gestured to the open air. "The voice that said, 'Makoto, rouse a sandstorm around us, now. Don't worry about me.' You didn't hear that?"

Makoto shook his head slowly as his eyes shot back to Ryu. "Maybe it was Ryu; but why didn't I hear him?"

Takeo shrugged. "I don't know, but if it was him, you should do it and we'll figure out later why I heard it and not you."

Makoto nodded and held out his hand, pointing it at Ryu, and the air started to move, slowly at first as not to rouse the enemy's attention, then all at once it ripped skyward, obstructing the warriors from sight.

Takeo pointed his hand at the sandstorm and added fire to the storm in front of them; what had at first been a gale turned to a gale of shattered glass. Makoto chewed on his bottom lip, but didn't say anything to Takeo as he worried about Ryu's safety; all other sounds died as they poured more and more power into their combined attack. A minute passed before a shadow descended on them, and Makoto gazed up into the disheveled face of Leonhardt. Before Leon could say a single word, Makoto shouted over the gale. "Ryu's battling two enemies in there!"

Leon nodded and pulled Makoto's sword from its sheath. At Makoto's protest Leon smiled his most devilish smile and bent down to his ear. "I'll bring this right back." Before he dived headfirst into the glass storm, he vanished from sight as the two kept up their combined attack.

Chapter Twelve:
The Warrior Within

The storm kicked up right as Ryu lunged forward, and his enemies vanished from sight right as he felt his sword sink into flesh. He jumped back and closed his eyes, expecting the dust to whip around him, but all he felt was the tug of air. He cautiously opened his eyes and found that the area around him for ten feet was calm. He uttered a low curse and whipped around, expecting one of his assailants to appear. *"That's not how I meant it! It was supposed to encompass all three of us!"*

He quickly changed his mind when the specs of dust turned to shards of glass and he heard twin howls of pain. *"That works."*

Kohaku and Zenaku emerged at the same time, both covered from head to toe in blood, and Ryu wasted no time in crossing blades with them. Zenaku's right arm hung limp at his side, and Kohaku had his left hand pressed against his stomach where a large piece of glass was sticking out. Zenaku stood behind Kohaku, and together they had their swords crossed in front of Kohaku's body. Ryu pushed them both back and a savage grin ripped across his face. "Now you both are weaker than me!" Ryu pushed them back step by step, until Zenaku grimaced as his back met the wall of glass. "You both will die here!" With one final shove Ryu threw Zenaku in the glass storm and watched as he flew with the storm, screaming in pain. Ryu turned his full attention to Kohaku, who was pushing back with all his might.

Ryu pushed himself bodily against Kohaku as he felt his power falter. "I've got you now Kohaku; you're gonna die for the year of hell you put me through!" Ryu knew without looking that his demon had receded to recover its strength. His arms were normal and his eyes were back to the white blue he was accustomed to. Just as Ryu could taste victory, he felt a searing pain in his back that made him leap to the side, away from Kohaku, and Ryu saw the source of his pain. A dimensional rift was opened right behind him, and the glass that had battered him was now ripping into Kohaku, who screamed with pain as he was pushed back into the storm. Ryu dropped to one knee, his strength gone, and he glanced up just as Kohaku was torn to shreds. His screams ended faster than Ryu would've liked, but he was glad he was gone.

Ryu's victory was short lived as Zenaku appeared from a second portal, blood pouring from multiple wounds on his body. But a pained grin was present on his face. "You think you can kill me?" Ryu tried to stand, but his legs gave out from underneath him and he collapsed again. "Cute plan. And the storm? Beautiful. I'll remember it next time I'm in a bad spot...I'm sure I can come up with some equivalent; maybe some sort of water/wind/ice combo. We'll see. Oh, I mean, *I'll* see. You, thankfully, won't be around to witness it."

He raised his sword arm and aimed it at Ryu's neck. "I'll cut the head from the beast and watch the body flop around, dead as you were the last time we fought. Goodbye. Demon."

The air whistled as Ryu bowed his head. His strength was gone; not even the threat of death could dissuade him. Calm settled over him. He had given his all, every ounce of strength his body and soul could muster. But, it wasn't

172

enough. Had it just been Zenaku he would've walked away the victor, but he just had to save his allies. *Even now they drag me down and cap my power...no, I still won. I fought both of my enemies and I won. Zenaku will not last the day with the wounds I've delivered. Sensei was right. I'm stronger with them than without.*

Ryu looked up into Zenaku's triumphant face and smiled; finally, he understood everything his sensei had tried to show him. And it was only when he looked death in the eye that he understood. Ryu blinked and heard Zenaku's sword cut the air. He felt blood splatter on his face, and the world went dark as he gave himself over before he could feel the pain. *"Sensei, I understand."* He hit the sand, unconscious, as a battle raged over him.

***

Leon burst through the glass storm behind Ryu as he closed his eyes. *Oh no you don't, you don't get to quit, not like that.* Leon ignored the blood dripping down his body as he ran behind Zenaku, crossed Makoto's sword in front of Zenaku, and caught his sword as he slid behind him and sank his fangs into Zenaku's neck. Zenaku screamed and started struggling, but Leonhardt had him in a vice hold that he couldn't break, and slowly, he stopped fighting. "Not like this, please let me fight!"

Leonhardt's eyes widened in surprise, but he didn't loosen his hold. "If I must die, let it be by a sword in my gut." Leonhardt would've grinned if he could've; he reversed Makoto's sword and impaled Zenaku on it.

The sword pierced through both of them as Leonhardt finally let go. Zenaku's head fell forward with a gasp. "That's not, what I meant."

Then he slumped, lifeless, next to Ryu's body. Leonhardt chuckled as he licked Zenaku's blood off Makoto's sword. "I have lived for this long because I have never shown mercy; I'm not gonna start with you." With one deft slice Zenaku's head was severed from his body. "And I was always taught to guarantee the kill with a decapitation or a torn heart, and since I doubt you have a heart, I'll take your head." With a swift kick he sent the head into the glass storm and watched it rip to pieces. Leon grinned as he walked over to Ryu and kneeled next to him.

"Ryu, you must awaken. It humbles me to say that I have no means of getting out of here without you."

Ryu stirred slightly, long enough to utter one word. "Stop."

The storm died instantly, and Leon looked over to Makoto and Takeo. "I do hope I didn't worry you two."

Takeo waved Makoto off and he bolted to Ryu's side. "Ryu, RYU! Don't even think about dying, you asshole." Takeo and Leonhardt looked at Makoto in surprise as Ryu stirred again. He placed one hand under himself and slowly pushed up.

"Don't curse; that's my thing, dick." He fell back on his haunches before standing up with his sword in hand. "I thought I was a goner. Who do I have to thank for keeping me among the living?"

Everyone turned to Leonhardt and Ryu groaned. "Should've just let me die." Leonhardt presented Fujin to Makoto, who took it and sheathed it with a smile.

Leon turned back to Ryu. "Next time, I might not save you if you continue to be so rude."

Ryu scoffed as he looked over to Takeo. "Well, if you could keep up, I wouldn't have to do all the work and save everyone...including myself."

Leonhardt shook his head. "I would never even dream of taking away the sport of it by always being on hand. Besides, that would deprive you of bragging rights." He chuckled as Ryu glared; before long Makoto joined in, and Ryu suddenly found the situation as humorous as the other two. Before any of them knew what happened, they were all laughing at nothing and everything. They would've continued longer, but Takeo's angry call had them all looking toward him. "Much as I hate to break this little humor circle, my leg *is* broken and I—"

He paled as a shadow fell over the three. Standing twenty feet from them was something only a nightmare could conjure. A monster that could only be called a demon stood before them, donned in all black armor; blue wisps like steam rose from the armor as the demon lifted a pure black sword over its head.

Without thinking, Ryu shoved Makoto and Leonhardt away from him just as the monster appeared before him, its sword descending faster than anything Ryu had ever seen before. He felt the sword bite into his skin, but he didn't feel the pain…just a numb cold, like someone had just run an ice cube over his left shoulder. The cold was all he felt as the thing's sword passed through him; he heard three gasps but had no idea why…the demon's sword hadn't hurt him. He turned to say as much, but froze as he kicked his own arm away, and he stared at it, stunned, as his eyes moved to the stump where his arm used to be. *No, this has to be a nightmare!* He commanded his arm to move like it would suddenly rise from a shroud, but nothing happened; he felt it out as blood shot out from the wound, but no arm appeared. Then he was gone and Tenma took over. He pulled the sword Kusanagi from its sheath as he slashed the air to his right. "Through the portal, NOW!"

Makoto and Leon ran toward the portal as Tenma kicked the severed arm at Takeo, who caught it, and Tenma appeared next to him. "Hold on to that." He sheathed Kusanagi and lifted Takeo with his remaining arm before throwing him over his shoulder. Just as he stood, he heard Takeo shout.

"On your left!" Tenma leapt to the right as a sword sliced into the earth, and then he bolted for the rift where Leon and Makoto had just gone. He passed through as he heard Takeo shout.

"It's right behind you!" Tenma put on a burst of speed

as he leapt through the portal, and with a single throw he sent Takeo flying towards the single point of light before running towards it himself, his internal alarms telling him stopping would result in his death. He dived forward and twisted in the air; the demon was less than a step behind him and closing fast. Right as he passed through the portal and slammed into the ground of Leonhardt's parlor, the demon passed through the portal as well. Without thinking, Tenma slashed his hand through the air and the portal slammed shut with the demon halfway through. Everyone stopped moving and held their breath for fear that it would start moving; then with an unearthly scream, it vanished in a cloud of black smoke, and everyone released a collective breath.

Tenma stood up and looked at everyone. "He's your problem now." His eyes changed back to white blue and Ryu fell to his knees. "What was that thing?" He spoke so softly that everyone missed half of what he said; when no answer was forthcoming, he spoke again, louder this time. "What the fuck was that goddamn thing?" The room was deathly silent, then someone spoke, someone who wasn't in their party.

"That, little brother, was the harbinger of horrible things to come."

Everyone turned toward the newcomer, who wasn't alone. Mitsuo, Takeshi, and Nori…all three stood at the door to Leonhardt's home.

"I know you wish to kill me, but if that truly was one of the Black Hand, then war is coming, and this world will need its champions…*all of them*."

Chapter 13:
Truce

Ryu had been treated, his severed arm now encased in a glass box, his torso wrapped in bandages. Takeo's leg was put into a splint, and now they all sat at the dining room table with Leonhardt sitting at the head, fully clothed in his usual attire. Ryu, Makoto, and Takeo sat side by side, and across from them were Mitsuo, Takeshi, and Nori. The air was still; no one spoke or breathed louder than was necessary. The only sound was Cassandra as she darted around, filling glasses with water...blood in Leonhardt's case. As she left the room, she whispered one last "thank you" to Makoto, then there were only the seven left.

Ryu was the first to make noise as he sighed, a very heavy sound that conveyed all his weariness in a simple gesture. "You three should speak, before I pass out from exhaustion." His voice was like grinding gravel, which spoke volumes about his missing arm as he kept shooting glances toward it. Mitsuo raised one brow before he lightly inclined his head.

"Very well; I had not expected the voice of reason to be you. But you're right...we are not here to provoke or battle with you. We are here about the demon that you just saw; an entity that has not been seen in fifteen years. The last time those monsters walked the earth, the world was plunged into

177

war and chaos the likes of which haven't been seen since feudal Japan and the Warring States Period." He paused to let his words sink in. Takeo and Makoto both turned toward Ryu, hoping for guidance, but his face was set in stone, so Mitsuo continued.

"During the last war, thousands were lost. Whole clans were wiped out. We won only because we forced the enemy to retreat through a portal that none of us could venture through in pursuit; we waited for weeks, but the enemy did not reemerge, so we declared ourselves the victors. Now they have returned, and before long we will be at war again. We need to use this time to gather our forces and strengthen our defenses."

Ryu stood up and everyone tensed, but he simply walked to the other side of the table and moved towards Mitsuo, who stood up and placed his hand on his sword. Ryu stood before him, now able to stand toe to toe with him. "What are the chances this was a freak occurrence?"

Ryu stared at his brother, their gazes level with one another, and Mitsuo responded simply. "None."

Ryu looked into his eyes for a full minute before he extended his hand. "Truce?"

If Mitsuo was surprised he didn't show it. He took Ryu's hand and shook it. "Truce."

Ryu pulled him close before whispering just loud enough for him to hear. "But our battle is far from over; when this is resolved you will fall before me."

Mitsuo chuckled as he walked back towards his team. "I'm looking forward to seeing your progress."

Ryu went back to his side of the table and sat down next to his teammates, who stared incredulously at him. Without a word Ryu spoke to them. "We need them; they've fought the enemy. They know what we have to do. I can handle small skirmishes, but a war is thousands upon thousands of opposition. They know what we have to face. More importantly, they know how to come out on top."

Ryu turned towards Mitsuo and laid his remaining arm on the table. "That being said, if this is some sort of ploy to kill us, you're gonna wish that demon, whatever it was, had succeeded the first time. Now, what's the plan?"

Mitsuo nodded. "We need the clans to unite; the elves, the fay, the werewolves, the vampires, the dragons, and all the others. In short, we need to rekindle all of the old alliances that were established when we fought the last war."

Leonhardt chose this moment to interrupt. "I can speak for the vampires and say you will not have our aid; we will not rally behind three men who can kill women and children and feel no remorse. That being said, the vampires will rally behind Ryu as the last true son of Oda."

Mitsuo seemed to flinch before he nodded. "Very well; this realizes a fear I have harbored. If my name is associated with this alliance, it would cut lifelines, so we will remain silent partners in this. Until the fighting starts, we will only act as guides."

Ryu nodded, feeling better and better about this by the second. "I will secure the werewolves, Makoto will work on securing the clans. I hope you kept records on who was sympathetic to our side of the war last time."

Mitsuo nodded, and it was Takeshi who spoke next. "I have hidden them; it will take some time to re-acquire them within the week, I believe."

Ryu stood up and moved to the door. "Then I guess we will reconvene in a week's time, to continue planning. Until that time I need to sleep. Leonhardt, will you provide them sanctuary?"

Leonhardt stood and moved around the table toward the door Ryu was about to exit through. "I will have to discuss it with the rest of my clan, but I see no reason why not."

Ryu opened the door and walked out, quickly followed by Takeo and Makoto, who was supporting Takeo. They went after Ryu and caught up to him just as he was about to shut the door to the rooms Leonhardt had given to them earlier. "Ryu, wait!"

Ryu sighed as he turned toward them. "What is it?"

Makoto seemed at a loss for words, so Takeo spoke for him. "What the hell was that...a truce? They killed our families; we can't just sweep that under a rug and forget about it!"

Ryu slammed the door and with his right arm, threw Takeo against the wall and held him there by his throat. Makoto stood shocked as Ryu glared at Takeo through the black soulless eyes he was learning to fear more and more every time he saw them. "Never think that I forgot, that I will ever forget that. But there are larger things at stake right now. If that truly was one of the Black Hand, then we are fast heading toward what could very easily be the end of life as we know it. So right now, the only reason I hate them for killing the Oda clan is the fact they took away a large resource of bodies. That's it! It's callous! And heartless! But this is war! We can't afford to be human and expect to survive; is that clear?"

He dropped Takeo and moved back to his door before looking over his shoulder at Takeo as he rubbed his throat, and Makoto who was helping him stand up. "You should get that rib looked at, before it gets worse."

He disappeared into his room as Takeo stared at the closed door in disbelief. Without a word he moved toward the door and pushed it open, closing it faster than Makoto could go after him. As soon as he moved to open the door Leonhardt's voice stopped him. "Let them work it out; I don't think you wish to be involved." Leonhardt grabbed him by the shoulders and led him away, as Makoto sent a prayer to Tsukiyomi that they wouldn't kill each other.

***

Ryu was lying down by the time Takeo burst through his door.

"How?"

Ryu shifted his head and looked at him as he uttered that

one word.

"How did you know?"

Ryu moved to look at the ceiling again. "I know for the same reason I can do this." There was a cracking sound and Takeo felt an intense itching sensation on his leg, followed by pressure on his ribs, before he put pressure on them both and didn't feel a lance of pain shoot up his leg or a knife stab in his ribcage. He stared at Ryu as Ryu moved toward the edge of the bed. He stood up, his leg buckling before another crack broke the silence, and then he was able to stand without any trouble.

"Somehow the bond switched and now I'm bonded to you."

Takeo backed up and pressed his back to the door as Ryu kept coming forward; something about the look in his eyes was making his heart race, and he knew it was his fight/flee instinct. But he knew that fighting was useless...he couldn't defeat Ryu. There was no other option; he opened the door and it slammed closed before he could leave. Then his mind registered a body pressed against his.

"Ryu, what are you doing?" He felt a hand press against his rapidly beating heart.

"I'm gonna ask you one time...if you say no, we will never speak of this to anyone; if you say yes, then you will be mine and I yours. So I ask: Will you give yourself to me, here and now?"

Takeo froze, and his heart skipped a beat. His stomach flipped on itself, and he spoke before he could think. "Yes."

Ryu closed his eyes...this was what he wanted; him and Takeo...him and his chosen. Without wasting anymore words, he grabbed Takeo's hand and led him to the bed, leaving a trail of clothes in their wake. Ryu pushed Takeo down on his back and lowered himself over his prone ally, teammate, lover, and mate. So many words, none of which could describe what they felt; years of misdirected love/hate, and now, they were finally able to focus it all to where it should've been from the beginning. To where *they* should've been since the beginning of it all; now they could be one.

***

Makoto followed Leonhardt as he led him through the castle, a grand tour long overdue, as Leonhardt had said. "And my sire. Count Dracula, who lost his life during the last war. Despite what TV and movies say, he was a great and passionate man, only feeding on humans who were judged to die by a jury of their peers."

He glanced over his shoulder and found that Makoto wasn't paying attention. "If I gave the tour without any clothes on, would that interest you, my dear Makoto?"

Makoto's gaze finally focused and he looked around, bewildered. "I'm sorry, what?"

Leonhardt chuckled as he turned around. "I asked: if I gave the tour naked, would you be more interested?"

Makoto blushed and looked away. "I'm sorry, I'm just worried."

Leonhardt nodded and led the way down more hallways before they came upon his private bedroom. He led Makoto in, sat him at his desk, and then sat on the bed. "My ear is all yours; what worries you?"

Makoto seemed to consider it, until finally, it all came out. "The war. Ryu. Takeo. Mitsuo. Nori. Takeshi. Everything. I'm worried about Ryu, because he's not acting like himself. He's here, but it's like he's a thousand miles away at the same time. And now with losing his arm, he seems even more volatile: and with Takeo, there doesn't seem to be anything that can get through to him. I can't talk to him, I can't even get him to look me in the eye. And now I'm worried that it's my fault for dragging Ryu into this; they never got along even before Ryu…went away, and then there's Mitsuo, Takeshi, and Nori. Who are in this castle and I don't know if they're genuinely in this, or if this is some kind of machination of theirs. And then there's you. I think I might be in love with you, but that can't be. Because me and

182

Ryu are supposed to be together, and you're a vampire. And, and, and."

His eyes swiveled to Leonhardt, who looked at him with an amused grin. Makoto stood up and moved toward the door. "And, I should go."

He opened the door but it only opened far enough for a foot to go through before Leonhardt's body stopped it and their eyes locked. "You think you *might* be in love with me? That's a pretty important *might*. So, when you figure it out, my door is always open to you."

He moved away from the door and Makoto held it ajar; he glanced over his shoulder and found Leonhardt sitting on the bed. "I think I've just figured it out." The door slammed shut at the exact moment that Makoto hit the bed, and Leonhardt's laughter filled the room.

Mitsuo still sat in the dining room with his teammates, a grin on his face. "My friends, this is the beginning of an alliance that will shake the very foundation of this world."

About the Author

I was home-schooled by my mom (also an author, Clarrissa Lee Moon), I am attending college now. I enjoy martial arts, swimming- anything physical actually. My dream is to either have a traditional home in Japan and open my own Dojo or maybe try my hand at being a Bounty Hunter or a Body-guard someday. My family encourages me to strive to be the best at anything I want to be and I still have a lot of time to figure that out. Right now, writing and college seems to be the thing to do now, so we will see what the future will bring later on.

www.ingramcontent.com/pod-product-compliance
Lightning Source LLC
Chambersburg PA
CBHW022114170626
46808CB00002B/731